# INFINITE INDIES 2023
## FORTRESS

INDIES UNITED PUBLISHING HOUSE, LLC
P.O. BOX 3071
QUINCY, IL 62305-3071
www.indiesunited.net

Infinite Indies
2020

Infinite Indies
2021

Infinite Indies
2022

*Dedicated to every person who ever took a chance on an unknown author.*
*Thank you.*

# Table of Contents

INDIES UNITED PUBLISHING HOUSE
PRESENTS

# Infinite Indies 2023

# FORTRESS

## A MULTI-AUTHOR ANTHOLOGY

INDIES UNITED PUBLISHING HOUSE, LLC

# FOREWORD

### Lisa Orban

The room is warm and inviting in a cluttered way, with books scattered around the woman sitting on a chaise lounge. She has a book in one hand and a warm beverage in the other; not far from her fingertips, an open box of goodies. A small smile is on her face as her eyes scan down the page, crinkling with hidden delight.

Looking up, she smiles, sets down the mug, puts a bookmark to hold her place, then gently closes the book. "Hello, please sit down." She waves at the overstuffed chair not far from hers. "Would you like to hear a story…?"

I love to tell stories. I always have. Put me in a room of one – or more – and I will spin tales designed to delight and sometimes horrify my audience, always leaving them wanting more. So, it's not surprising that one day in 2015, I sat down to write some of the stories I had been telling my whole life. Now I could share my adventures not only with random strangers and close friends, but with anyone who picked up one of my books anywhere in the world.

Not many years after that, with the help of Jennie Rosenblum, the world's greatest cheerleader, I opened Indies United Publishing House so other authors could share their stories with the world. What a ride it has been! Armed with a lot of knowledge and unflappable enthusiasm, I attempted something never done before; I opened a publishing house that put authors before all else. To build a community within the writing world that was supportive and collaborative. Nurturing and guiding the many voices that walked through our doors, giving them all equal consideration and footing.

As you now know, I love stories—particularly short stories, where you can jump in and romp to the end in a single gulp. There is something special about creating a short story: to grab your reader and hold them completely enthralled, to develop entire worlds and characters with a few broad strokes and, most importantly, make your readers feel for those characters with that brief peek into their lives.

In 2020, Indies United published our first short story anthology, Infinite Indies 2020, and released a new one every year since. They were wide ranging, include every genre, poetry, and even commentary articles on writing. A grab-bag of literature, if you will.

But, this year I decided to do something different. Inspired by an article I read about the late, great John Campbell of Astounding. Campbell was known for fostering some of the greatest science fiction writers we know today, giving them a place to tell their stories and challenging them to hone their skills. One challenge was to come up with individual stories using the concept phrase, *goldfish bowl*. When finished, he published those stories together launching the careers of several now well-known authors.

Gathering my authors, I gave them a similar challenge. Write a story based on a single word, *FORTRESS*. Take it in any direction you want, but run with it. And run they did. Each story in this book reflects the writer's perception of the word, from the dark depths of despair to the elusive mystical.

We present to you *Infinite Indies: Fortress*. So, curl up in your favorite chair with your beverage of choice and enjoy this literary charcuterie board of small delights.

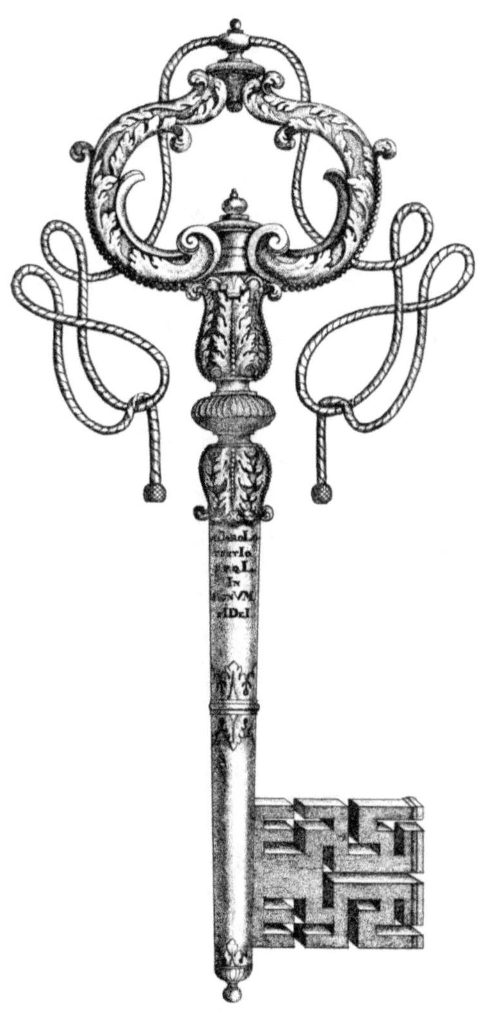

# Crumbling Towers

## Marie Judson

Trifena Findern's eyes glazed over as she struggled to write a scholarly article on medieval bardic texts. The topic had been riveting when she'd started researching. Now, on the eighteenth revision, her gaze drifted out the glass doors of her graduate apartment's balcony toward towering eucalyptus trees, "ghost gums" as her Australian friend, an art therapist, called them. In a rising wind, they hovered, swaying like shaggy giants, over the canyon.

Her fingers went rogue and wandered to e-mail, where she spotted a post from her sci fi fantasy group. "I'll just check and see," she told herself, while a small voice chided her for abandoning scholarly focus.

"Dreaming of running off with Travelers?" Indigo teased in an email, from her Melbourne home.

"How'd you know?" Tref shot back and was about to

embellish on that favorite topic when her screen went black. Yanking her hands from the keyboard, she prayed she hadn't lost her latest draft.

Like a slow fade in a slideshow, an image took shape on the screen: two crumbling towers on a cliff, backed by charcoal clouds.

Tref had never seen this place, but it gave her a jolt, as if triggering a lost memory.

Then she found herself engulfed in inky nothingness, feeling neither body nor breath; she'd turned to icy smoke.

Next instant, she stood in a pummeling wind, mist whipping past; her apartment was nowhere in sight. Damp penetrated her thin yoga pants and flannel shirt and she hugged her arms around her, rubbing salt from her eyes. She dimly made out two crumbling towers, showing in and out of the moving mist. Gulls cried out, and waves thundered, pummeling the cliffs beyond.

She started toward the towers; they'd at least block the brutal wind. As she pushed forward, teeth chattering, a tall caped figure materialized from the fog next to the stone ruins.

Tref's heart raced. She glanced behind her but there was nowhere to go, only mist and tall grasses. Turning back, she saw that the stranger had spotted her and gestured wildly for her to approach. There was little option; the bare headlands offered no shelter. Besides, she felt herself drawn toward the hooded person's urgency, as if compelled. She hurried forward, pushing against the stinging wind, slapping palms at her eyes to clear her vision.

The strange, gaunt figure stepped forward and pressed a flat bag into her hands, hissing, "Quick! Keep it safe. Do not let *anyone* get it away from you." The voice was deep and raspy but could have been a woman's. It was hard to tell. Deep in the shadows of the hood, intense eyes peered out. Then the mysterious caped form whirled and vanished around the towers, into the thickening mist.

Racing to follow, Tref called, "What do you mean? What is this? Who are you?" Reaching the rounded wall, she stared around but saw no one.

She stood staring into the mist, pressed to the stone wall until shivers wracked her. She moved along the tower side until she came to a doorway. Grateful for protection from the wind, she nearly fell into the interior, but rain began to fall and she realized the tower had no roof.

In the fading light, she tugged at the knot on the bag but it was tight and her fingers were stiff with cold. She explored the flat cloth and discovered hard objects within. An old key? A tiny hammer? A marble? It was hard to tell for sure.

Night was falling swiftly and this tower would offer little protection from the rain. She crossed to the second tower to find it was equally roofless, walls jagging into the blustering sky. Thunder cracked and rain fell in fat drops. A doorway faced the sea and she stood in its shelter, scanning the shoreline. She thought she caught a faint glimmer of light, coming and going in tendrils of fog. A tavern? Welcoming home or a den of thieves? She could not know. What she did know was she was alone in a roofless fortress without supplies.

Was this a dream? If so, it felt very real and very cold. And daylight had disappeared. She made a decision, stepped away from the tower's scant protection and crossed to the cliff edge. Kneeling, she gazed over, assessing a possible descent to shore. Though treacherous, the cliff seemed scalable. The problem was the last part; it curved under and she could not see how much of a drop it would be onto rocks before she could get to the beach.

Gathering resolve, she flopped onto her belly on stoff sea grasses and slid her legs over the side. Her toes, in thin wet socks, found roots. She let her weight onto them and searched for handholds in crumbling sandstone. Shaking with cold, she found a ledge, then another, and slid, scraping, downward, scraping arms and knees.

When she came to the last shelf, she peeked over and spotted only wave-dashed rocks below. There was one spot where she could drop onto kelp, if she had the nerve. With little option and no time, she crouched and leaped. One bruised knee, but she was down. However, she found herself surrounded by water and the beach looked farther away than it had from the top. Night was swiftly encroaching. With a deep breath, she started to scramble across rocks, navigating tidepools, climbing crags. Jamming salt-weighted hair out of her eyes, she stopped and calculated the best way to shore. In the thick fog, she could only see a single strip of stone between her and the beach; she'd have to wade to it and hope it was shallow on the far side.

She stepped into the freezing water. A wave struck her but she floundered to the next strip of rock. By now it was so dark, she had to feel her way, clinging to rocks' slick surfaces. She squeezed into a crevice between two stones, climbed upward, madly, and at last found herself dropping onto coarse sand at the shoreline.

Feeling an elation of achievement, she plummeted through waves that battered and sucked at her, soaked clothes weighing her down. At the shallow edge, she dropped to hands and knees, exhausted.

The dark beach stretched away from her. She couldn't

stay out there long. She pushed shakily to standing and took stock again, searching anxiously for the light she'd seen—or thought she'd seen—from the cliffs above. Salt caked and burned in her eyes as she peered down the coast, seeing no flicker of light.

The beach was narrow, bordered by dark woods. At least they would break the wind and rain. Summoning strength, she dashed that way, feet feeling like numb stumps hitting the coarse wet sand. At the forest's edge, she pressed gratefully in between trees, branches scratching. One more time, at this slightly higher vantage, she gazed down the coastline, rubbing her eyes with a wet sleeve.

In lulls in the wind, she thought she heard music deeper in the forest. With the wind howling, it was impossible to tell what direction the sound came from, though. She stared into the dark. Would it be wise to plunge into the forest following strains of music? Any smarter to keep to the shore chasing glimpses of lights? At least under the trees she had shelter. She could angle parallel to shore.

She felt for the bag, which she'd ended up shoving mostly into her yoga pants. Somehow through her struggles down the cliff and over rocks, through waves, to shore, she'd kept it safe. What was even in it to cause such desperation in the stranger's voice and countenance, as if it held the fate of the world in its thin contents. Why did she feel responsible for it now? Why was she entrusted with it, for that matter? And how would anyone expect her to show up in that deserted place. Unless… it had been very strange, the way she'd come to be there. The blackness, the feeling of nothingness.

Fumbling again to open it, she gave up and tucked it

again, her shirt covering where it flapped over. Teeth doing a mariachi, thin shirt and pants clinging, feet aching, she hugged a tree trunk, unable to decide where to proceed, or even if she could forge a way through the dense forest.

Just then, a raven fluttered onto a branch above her head, landing clumsily, buffeted by wind, and cawed. It was so close that its black showed against gray all around as it tilted a beady eye toward her, then flew a short distance away, deeper into the woods and landed again, hunching against the wind that buffeted the tree tops.

She took a certain comfort in another living creature.

The bird seemed to wait for her. It cawed toward her, insistent. Not wanting to lose connection yet, she followed, though this wasn't the direction she'd planned. Twigs gouged her cold feet as she picked her way gingerly among the trees.

Over and over, the raven took off, landed deeper in the woods, and turned to face her, yelling its raucous cry. She rushed to keep up with her guide, wondering all the while if she should have kept near shore. She wanted to think some kindly fate had sent the bird to lead her to safety. At the same time, a nervous thought tugged at the back of my mind, warning her not to be dragged out of sight of the place where it started. The crumbling fortress.

She'd come this far, figuring it held promise, though that promise had been a twinkle of light she no longer could see. She kept moving so as not to lose the raven. The forest floor climbed in a slight incline, then rose in a steeper ascent. The raven landed way in front of her, at the highest point she could see, then took flight. With a hard scramble, she came out of the trees and barely caught herself on a sapling at a cliff's edge on a ridge looking out over treetops. Wind struck her and she backed up until she crouched under low trees. Below, lights glowed on a valley floor. She heard the music again, and now voices carried fitfully up on the wind.

Settling cross-legged, she watched, trying to make out who might be down there.

"Not too quiet, are we?" A man's voice came, soft and low, from a few feet away.

Tref's head jerked around, heart battering against her ribs.

A man stood casually against a nearby tree in a heavy cape and boots. The raven stood on his shoulder.

"Not as quiet as you, surely, sneaking up on people," she said with some rancor.

He grinned.

"Did you train your bird to lead me to you?" she asked then, suspicion growing.

At this, he threw back his head and shouted with laughter.

From below, a voice called up, "Vadi, who are ye playin' with in the woods? Come down and help or I'll spit ya over th' fire instead of whatever Domi brought in. What is this, Domi? It's got fur. That's all I can tell!"

Voices in the hollow below laughed and bantered.

"Now's your chance, Little Rabbit," the man said softly. "Do ye bolt, or do ye join us?"

She started to get up but sat again, clothes catching on brambles, and squinted up at him, trying to judge his character. For a minute or two, the rain had dwindled, but now it pelted harder. Reaching under her shirt, she felt the bag, wondering if anything in it could be used as a weapon. If she swung it very hard? Being an academic, she knew mainly about things in books, not the mind in the wild. Certainly not how to wield a weapon.

"Come," Vadi said, holding out a hand. "Our warm fire and whatever food is being mustered down there can surely serve you better than whatever you have stored under that shirt."

She yanked her hand from under her shirt. How had he seen that? Was he a wizard? She wavered, indecisive. What was she to do? If he wanted to hurt me, he certainly could, whether she walked with him voluntarily or tried to run. At least she could be gracious, in case his intentions were honorable. Besides, by now, delectable smells wafted up to her from the camp below.

She grasped his big, warm hand with her cold, sandy one and he pulled her to standing, chuckling as he unhooked a briar strand from her shirt. She felt him studying her thin clothing and stocking feet with faint amusement.

She pulled her hand away and crossed her arms, self-conscious. "Must you stare?"

He chuckled. "I'm trying to imagine what hamlet you wandered from, out into this weather with…" he paused, seeming to search for words, settling on, "such apparel." Subtly, he brushed his hands off on his rugged trousers as he led the way down a faint deer path. He turned occasionally to see if she needed help with difficult places where their feet careened down soft soil or roots tried to trip them.

At the base of the hill, a path led into the camp, which she could now see was large and buzzing with activity under bright tents. Loud conversation blended with the sounds of music, chopping and general camp noises. Children ran and laughed.

They arrived at a canopy stretched over a small

clearing, providing shelter for dinner preparation. Wavering torches lit the underside of the canvas which was covered in painted scenes that rippled in the fitful winds, giving the images an unreal look, almost like an animation. Brown faces turned toward her where she stood next to Vadi, teeth chattering.

Suddenly laughing women surrounded her, clucking and muttering, giving Vadi sideways glances and scolding in a tongue she didn't recognize. This made her wonder how she'd known what the men called up from below.

The women pulled her out of sight between blankets and peeled off her wet clothing, for which she was grateful. They tsked over her scrapes and bruises. A plump woman with a musky scent dobbed salve on and some pain stopped, while some grew worse before it dwindled away.

Before long, she stepped out bundled in layers of skirts, shirts and shawls. Woolen socks met thick leggings. Fur lined boots came halfway up her calves.

She was drawn to the central fire and handed a warm mug which comforted her insides, as her outside now felt heavenly. Seated on a log between warm bodies, she ate thick stew grateful to fill her belly. She'd not been gone from home all that long but had worked up a hearty appetite.

Men, women, and youth danced in colorful clothing in the space next to the fire. Musicians played and drank in equal parts, it seemed, trading banter with dancers and onlookers.

Tref gulped steaming, spiced brew, sweet and yeasty, then set it between my boots to eat more thick stew. Her teeth had stopped chattering and the heady drink careened through her with a giddy burn. Bites of turnip, seafood and wild herbs settled her uneasy nerves into a growing glow of contentment. She ate it all, set down the bowl and hugged the hot drink, watching dancers whirl on the packed earth, savoring the swirl of color, the serenade of foreign sounds and scents of unfamiliar spices. She could no longer tell if rain pattered outside the tent.

"Have another." A woman refilled her cup.

*Was it a good idea to become inebriated?* she asked herself. But the first round had rendered her incapable of caution. She smiled at the gap-toothed woman and gulped the fermented brew with its curious resiny aftertaste.

A woman on one side of her shifted to take Tref's hand.

"I'm Sanda." Her voice was deep and rich, her gaze mesmerizing. Long black hair streaked with silver fell forward as Sanda peered at Tref's palm. The Traveler glanced up through her fringe.

Was it the drink that made her feel mesmerized? "I'm Tref." Her words sounded slurred to her own ears.

Sanda searched her face closely. "Hmmm…" she said, with doubt in her voice. As if seeking a second opinion, she again concentrated on Tref's palm, brows furrowed. She traced the lines, mouth pressed into deep caves.

*This is too much. Now a Traveler palm reading?* In truth, she'd always wanted one.

A man knocked into her legs as he passed, dancing. He turned and, gripping her shoulder for balance, bowed deeply. "A thousand… apologies." His lips, inches from her face, were dark red, finely formed. He grinned, revealing brilliant teeth, only one or two missing. One in front gleamed gold in the torchlight.

She grinned, despite the painful grip, unable to resist his grand gesture. He moved off into the dancers. As her eyes followed him, he leaped lithely and winked at her.

"Hmph," Sanda snorted. "Watch out fer that one." She continued to trace palm lines, mumbling, until at last she grinned and straightened, placing Tref's hand back in her lap. "It's all clear now."

"Is it?" Tref asked. "What's clear?"

"Why you've come."

With that very cryptic remark, Sanda pushed up from the log and left.

Tref stared after her. "You know why I came?" She wanted to run after her but found her legs were wobbly.


Morning light jabbed Tref's eyes. She felt soft bedding, like flannel, around her. Cracking her eyes carefully to avoid stabs of pain, she tried to study the small, brightly decorated interior of what appeared to be an enclosed wagon. She did not recall how she'd gotten there.

As she pushed to sitting, her stomach reeled.

At that moment, a girl, maybe twelve years old, hair in two long braids, entered through curtains that divided the space. She knelt and offered Tref a steaming cup that smelled strange.

Tref propped on an elbow, head slamming. Rays of light felt like screwdrivers running through her temples. She pushed the drink away and lay back down but the girl shook her head. "Nay. Drink it. It'll help."

Gamely, Tref took a tiny sip and scowled.

The girl laughed and nodded. "I know. Last summer I et somethin' bad and Nana made me have it, too. Tastes somethin' awful but really does help."

A quavering voice called from the other side of the curtain. "Zafi! Did she drink it?"

The girl giggled without sound, then called, "She's

drinkin', Nana."

Tref took another sip, nearly gagging and pushed it away again.

"If swallow it all down, you realy will feel better. I promise." She glanced at the curtain, as if afraid not to get it all into their visitor.

A clawed hand grasped the heavy cloth divider, and a withered face pushed through, followed by a bent figure swathed in a black shawl with bright birds and fish stitched on it. Approaching, the old woman scowled, tapping her cane against the floor by the bed.

Tref pulled the cup back and took a large gulp, trying not to grimace.

The roiling in her stomach eased and the pounding in her head reduced to light timpani. She nodded at the hawk-like stare.

Satisfied, the girl's nana slowly turned and moved back into her inner sanctum.

When Tref had managed to down the last of the bitter drink, the girl took the cup and disappeared into the back.

Tref scooted back against pillows and gazed around. Small windows opened onto trees, branches waving in a light breeze. Shelves, secured by rope netting, held a variety of interesting objects: feathers poked from old books, a satin flower dangled out of a jar alongside tarnished forks and knives, a carved box, a tiny man carved of oak, dressed in perfect shiny shirt and pants. Drawstring bags caught her eye and she remembered the one entrusted to her.

Sitting up, her eyes traveled the room, searching for her clothes. They had been taken off of her by the women. She had no idea which women.

She scrambled from bed and searched in cupboards

and drawers. Finding no sign of anything belonging to her, she called out, "Zafi?"

The girl came through, carrying a stack of clothing. But they were not hers.

"Do you know where my things are?" Tref asked. "Women helped me get my wet things off last night but I'm not sure where they ended up."

The girl pointed outside.

Tref started toward the painted outer door but Zafi stopped her with a gentle hand on her arm. "You should put these on."

Tref remembered she was still wearing the nightgown she had mysteriously awoken in. She accepted the embroidered skirt and peasant blouse, underthings, slip-on shoes, and light shawl and changed.

Dressed in borrowed clothes, she stood at the top of the wagon stairs, looking out at the sun-lit camp. Where had the storm gone? Wagons were interspersed with pale-leaved trees. She descended and jumped off the bottom step, breathing in campfire air. Blue skies showed between branches above.

She wandered, gazing at wagons and the groups gathered near them.

She'd slept in a Traveler camp, she thought with wonder, not letting her thoughts go further to how she'd gotten there, lest she doubt her sanity.

Camp sounds filled the air.

By the third or fourth caravan, she spotted, on a rope stretched to a tree, her plaid shirt and yoga pants flapping in the breeze, along with her underclothes, for all to see. Hurrying over, she started to take them off the line, in the process searching for the bag.

"We don't have it," a woman said from the top step.

Did everyone know about her bag? "You don't... then who does?" Tref felt anxious as she rolled her underthings into her shirt and pants.

The woman—Tref thought her name might be Vandya —pointed.

Tref followed the line of her finger toward where the camp seemed to end, then shrugged with lifted brows. "What? Where?"

"The Magician," was all Vandya said before she re-entered the cabin on wheels and shut the door.

Tref stood, undecided. Where was Vadi this morning? She decided to walk through camp to look for him. Maybe she wouldn't have to approach this "magician" alone.

Tents and canopies had been taken down to let in the sun. Wagons–some rounded, others square, some painted, others plain—had all their wooden covers and doors open to let through the fresh air and warmth.

Groups she passed called greetings and offered food. She waved and nodded but passed on.

*What would the magician be like?* She came to the clearing where the music and dancing had been and realized she had arrived at the other side of where Vandya had pointed. In a small clearing of its own stood a magnificent wagon, taller than most, covered in *trompe de l'oeil* designs that made its sides seem to twist and bend as she approached. It had a grand location above a stream. Two immense horses grazed close by.

At the end of the wagon facing her sat a huge man with a puffy black beard and hair like a cloud. He smirked in her direction; the velvet bag stretched across his lap. "Not the one t' be trusted with somethin' valuable, are ye?" he said as she drew close.

His bright eyes seemed to take her in completely and,

at the same time, look right through her.

"Here y' are." A woman stepped up behind her. "My clothes look well on y'. But we sh'd do somethin' with yer hair."

Tref wondered, then, what chaos sat upon my head.

The saucy woman, whose clothes she apparently wore, seemed in her twenties, with a luxuriant figure well displayed in a low draping blouse and a skirt that hugged her hips.

"Oh, these are yours?" Tref felt embarrassed. "Are you... is that your mother's wagon I slept in?"

"Grand aunt. Grandmother. I don't know. Luludja fostered me. I see ye've found Tazi, our Knot Master. That bag's 'll try only the least of his tricks."

Everyone *does* know about my bag. Tref felt a rising panic.

"Don't be so sure, Mirela," The smirky giant said. "Seems bespelled, this one."

No wonder she hadn't been able to open it. She felt just the slightest bit better about herself.

Mirela folded her arms. "Ye canno' get it open? But ye know what's in it."

"How?" She looked from one to the other. "You mean, by feeling it?"

"He can see." Mirela stared at Tref like she had the mind of a three-year-old. "He's blind, ye know, but he sees what others can't. Well, I have things to do." Mirela whirled and swaggered away, her shapely figure swaying in its bright, swishy skirt with each step.

"But your clothes," Tref called.

"You keep 'em for now. You can't wear ... those." Mirela pointed at the balled-up garments tucked under Tref's arm.

Tazi stood, towering over her. "Why don't ye want me t' get it open?" He was so tall she looked straight at his stomach.

"It's just that…" I stammered, talking to his middle button.

"Just that…?" He looked down over his bushy black beard at the top of her head.

How much should she tell him? Why should she keep that strange person's secret? She would need allies to get home. Or just to survive. She decided to take a chance. Squinting up at the man's face far above her, she said, "The… uh… person who gave it to me said—"

"Who?" The man pushed her back to see her face, hands engulfing her shoulders gently.

He sat again. "See this?" He took up a snarled tangle of rope from under his wagon. Laying it on his lap, he spoke over it. Slowly the strands moved, slithering along their paths like a pile of snakes, slipping apart until the whole mass lay in neat parallel lines across his massive thighs.

"Wow, that's… impressive." Suddenly aware of just how powerful this man was, she glanced around her. "Where's Vadi this morning?" She tried to ask casually. It wasn't as though she knew the other man well. But this writhing rope thing had her feeling off-kilter.

"Vadi's gone," the man said, his voice a deep rumble in his chest. He did not seem displeased to make the announcement as he stared toward a road winding out of the valley and disappearing into the distance.

"He's gone?" she whispered. "Where?"

Tazi shrugged.

Tref held out her hand for her bag.

Taz shook his big shaggy head. "I'll hold onto it for now."

And that was that. Tref walked away, absolutely sure she was no match for this man, and frankly a bit relieved to let the bag go. Curious about her hair, she made for Luludja's wagon, where she'd slept, and climbed the steps. "Zafi?"

The girl's face appeared in the open upper half of the doorway.

"I have salt-caked hair," Tref said.

Zafi glanced up and stifled a laugh, hand over her mouth. "You want to bathe?"

"Also I need to put these somewhere til I can wash them." Tref held her bundle of clothes.

"Gramma will boil them."

"Oh, I can do it." Tref was eager not to be a burden, and wasn't sure what boiling would do to her favorite plaid shirt.

As they walked along the stream, Zaf prattled on about everything from clan gossip to her beliefs about fairies. "This is why we like to camp here," she said lifting a frond to expose a small pool with steam rising from its surface. "It's warm."

Since they had the place to themselves, they stripped and jumped in.

Zafi had brought a bag with a foaming cake to wash hair and they spent a glad hour splashing around, washing, then lying out in the sun on a blanket, hidden by tall grasses, before dressing again. They put braids in each other's hair and even stuck little wildflowers into strands roped over their heads, held in with clasps Zafi'd brought. Tref had not spent such a sublime day since... well, probably since childhood, playing with her sister.

In the evening, as Tref sat with others under the stars, nibbling at something roasted, horse's hooves sounded on the road.

"Vadi's back!" someone called. "Maybe he'll play. I'm tired of yer fiddlin', Gordo."

"Fine then. I'll go slit my throat." The man who must be Gordo showed no rancor after such dire words as he headed for a barrel of drink and filled his cup, swiftly foaming his mustache with the contents.

A short while later, Vadi emerged from the shadows wearing a clean, dark red shirt, his hair neatly combed and tied back. She hardly recognized him as he stood eating and drinking with a cluster of men. His eyes caught Tref's and he nodded, the barest acknowledgment.

"Play, Vadi!" someone shouted, and others chorused in.

He set down his plate and, keeping his mug of drink, joined the musicians. He laid a worn bag across his lap and drew out a mandolin of surpassing beauty. It caught firelight on its polished, inlaid wood. He held it with tenderness, like a lover. Unhurried, he stroked his first notes. The other musicians grinned and moved into the melody, sad and beautiful. It pulled Tref's soul with it.

The music shifted to a dance reel, then to a ballad. She enjoyed each sound until Vadi set his mandolin gently aside, walked to her and sat.

Close up, in the firelight, his face was appealing, neither young nor old. She liked the serious lines as well as the laughing ones. Yet this was not a man to take lightly. There was something in his eyes... they could go from mocking to threatening, it seemed.

"And how have ye passed yer day?" he asked. His eyes took her in from the hair to the clothes. "I see they've outfitted ye. You look very different from last night." His face stayed sober, betraying nothing.

"I've been well cared for," she said.

"I like your hair," he added with a glint in his eyes.

"Oh, are the flowers still there? Zafi—" she reached up but he stopped her hand.

"Don't take them out."

She stopped and their eyes met, his hand still holding hers. Flummoxed, she said, "I never thanked you."

"Thanked me? For what?"

"For saving me. Bringing me here." Then she thought about what she'd said, about the raven, asking had he trained it to bring her. But instead of apologizing, she asked, "Where's the raven?"

Vadi's inscrutable eyes gazed at her, then glanced around at his clan, laughing and talking. "Walk with me a moment." He stood.

Puzzled, she got up, too. She felt the gazes of the others as they walked away into a dark meadow. The evening was growing chilly. She pulled the shawl close around and admired myriad stars.

"I hear there's a mysterious bag that's of some interest," Vadi began quietly.

"Ah. Yes. Tazi has it."

Vadi took her shoulders and pressed his mouth to her ear. "It must not stay here."

Shivers ran down her as his breath tickled her neck, stirring a visceral response.

But she pulled back to look at him. What was the interest in this bag? What was at stake? Did she really owe more allegiance to the one who'd given it to her than to these Travelers? How could she know? She had so little information. And was that gaunt individual planning to find her and retrieve it? How? "What do you know?" she asked at last.

"Know...?"

"Why should it not stay here? Who should it go to? What do you know about it?" Normally a rather reclusive and peaceful person, Tref was finding her failure to meet her original obligation to cause a strange fierceness in her. Maybe that hooded person by the crumbling towers had put a spell on her as well as the knot tying the bag.

"I only know it is not safe here. For it? For us? I don't know."

"But... what is it?"

They were whispering, standing so close Tref smelled horse musk, smoke, and soap on the man, along with the yeasty beer on his breath.

"And where should it be instead?" she added.

A cracked twig made them stop talking and listen for sounds around them.

She imagined it would be hard to get the drop on Vadi. She could feel him sensing around them as, not far away, the happy sounds of the camp continued on—shouts, whistles, a baby crying.

Again, he brought his lips close to her ear and his voice was as soft as wind in a tree. "There is a council of elders. We'll ride to them tomorrow. For tonight, I will sleep near your wagon."

"But," she started to repeat, "I don't have it. Ta—"

He put a finger on her lips and shook his head, whispered, "There's a reason it was given to you. You also are ... part of it. Related to it."

The feel of his finger on her lips made it hard to sort the many questions that flew around inside her head. What did he mean about her being part of it? And did he not trust Tazi? Whose plan was this, to take the bag elsewhere? And where had he gone today?

"Come. You're shivering," he said, a hand on her shoulder.

She was, and it wasn't all the cold of the night. They returned to the fire. Vadi did not play his mandolin again.

He was as good as his word and stayed close that night. They slept on cots by Mirela's caravan. Tref tried not to wonder about the relationship between Mirela and Vadi.

When she mentioned needing to relieve herself, Vadi sent Mirela with her and followed at a distance. "You hear a crack, a breath, anything unexpected, you call my name," he instructed.

"Aye, aye, *capitan*." She saluted.

He stared at her blankly. Tref had a dawning feeling that they were not speaking English, she included.

Walking at Mirela's side, Tref said, "Thank you for coming with me," carefully listening to discern what language she spoke.

"*Djokh?*" It was a protest, not a question. "Why do you speak the language of the others?"

"What are we speaking?" Tref asked. She felt Mirela's shrug in the darkness at her shoulder.

"Ye've been speakin' it all day. Don't ye know?"

"I don't think I knew your language before yesterday," Tref said honestly, with growing confusion.

"Maybe you're one of those that *know* things."

What did she mean? Like read minds? Well, she never knew it, if that was the case.


Next morning, early, Vadi walked across camp toward Tref leading two horses.

Zafi and Mirela had outfitted Tref with thick leggings, unrestrictive skirts and quilted jackets.

She mounted a horse with Vadi's help.

"This is Night Whisper," he said, stroking the strangely dappled horse's shoulder.

They climbed the long hill out of the Traveler camp with only blankets on the horses. Tref's inner thighs were definitely not used to prolonged contact with horses' coats and girths. They already began to chafe and she wondered how far they'd ride.

When they reached the ridge that overlooked the coast, she saw a cliff with two towers. But they were whole, with battlements built around them. She shivered. Maybe they were different towers. The field looked the same, though now it was struck by sunlight. The cliff appeared surprisingly sheer from there. How had she managed? She studied the rocks below. It was hard to tell from here. But if it wasn't the same place, how would she find her way back?

She studied the narrow beach she'd crossed and looked the other way to try to see what light she might have seen. She trotted up next to Vadi. "I saw a light that way, the night you found me."

"Did ye?" They both squinted the shore. "Mayhap an encampment." He frowned, scrutinizing the stretch of land below them.

"I climbed down that cliff, planning to follow the light, to find people and shelter. But then I didn't see it anymore. That's when I went into the woods, to get out of the rain."

"That might not ha' been safe." He squinted sideways at me.

"Well, how'd I know you'd be safe?" she asked with a

crooked smile.

"Ya didn't." He gave me a wicked grin. "Maybe I'm not."

Her stomach flipped but she decided to ignore it. "Then your raven found me." She watched his face to see if he'd give anything away. But he only peered down the coast a last time, then turned to trot along the ridge, the sea to their right, away from the towers.

"It led me through the woods," she went on, following behind him on the narrow trail. "I thought I heard music but it was hard to tell with the storm."

They rounded a bend and wind lashed them.

"Why do I understand your language?" She shouted to be heard.

"Ye may have the *Knowin'*." He looked at me speculatively.

"That's what Mirela said." It seemed a common idea with this group.

He pointed ahead. "See the dark mountain. Furthest that way?"

Her heart sank. Already her legs felt rubbed raw and it was still morning.

"That's where I was born," he said.

"That's not where we're going now?"

"Oh, nay." He laughed and pointed to the coast, a ways further down from where they were. "We head to a sea cave near that hamlet. We'll be there by midday."

She let out a sigh of relief.

Vadi laughed.

They heard a hawk's peeerrrr as it plummeted straight toward them from high in the sky. Vadi grabbed her reigns and dashed down a ravine, squeezing them and their horses under an overhanging rock just before the great bird swooped, talons out. It landed on the roadside, turned, eyed them, then flapped violently back into the sky, winging away.

They had to go forward to find a path back onto the road. There, Vadi kicked his horse and they set off in a cantor, barreling along to a road that descended toward the coast.

He veered suddenly between trees, and they were pushed, scratched and lashed by branches, into woods that headed away from the sea.

Tref stayed close, grateful that she's had some horseback riding lessons as a kid.

They kept on way, pressing through dense woods, until at last he came to a stop and waited for her to come alongside. "Sorry," he said, touching a scratch on her cheek. "I didn't want to stay in the open."

She nodded. "What was that bird? Did it actually attack us?"

He held up a hand for her to wait. Soon the path disappeared and they again wove through trees, less dense this time, until they came out on a wide trail. Limbs crossed overhead, forming a sun-dappled avenue. The raven landed on Vadi's shoulder.

Tref thought she'd seen it at times along their journey. She watched in astonishment as the Traveler took the bird's head in his hand and seemed to speak against its feathers. It jerked away and took off as they entered a cave. They stayed mounted until the roof was too low to ride, then climbed off and walked the horses through narrow, winding passages, often splitting off from other tunnels.

Tref grew worried. "I wouldn't want to lose my way in here." Her voice echoed.

"It's not much farther." Vadi had no problem navigating through the dark.

They turned a bend, and an arch filled with sunlight appeared before them. They stepped out into a tiny meadow. Bees buzzed. Tref squinted in the bright light.

"You know this land well, don't you?" she commented.

Vadi nodded and whistled a birdcall. An identical call answered and Tref followed Vadi through a thin forest to a small marsh. In the middle a deep pool welled up, with indigo water, fed by a low waterfall. Flowers dotted grasses and moss. A man with long white hair and beard stepped into the sunlight on the far side and waved. His long robe was bright blue. Something shiny on it caught the light with bright sparks.

They stepped through lush, velvety grasses. They crossed a small stream, stepping on large flat stones to reach the old man and left the horses happily munching herbage.

Up close, Tref saw that the venerable man wore layered robes in shades of blue from pale to indigo, worn but clean. A creature popped its head out of his beard. A baby otter. He stroked it. The tiny thing leaped out and scampered into the water. The stream wandered through the grotto into a dark cave mouth. Birds' chirping filled the air.

"Lumin." Vadi said as he embraced the wise looking man.

"It's been too long," Lumin said.

"I had not meant it to be so," Vadi answered.

"Come. Sit."

They settled on rocks covered in soft, dry moss, Tref in the middle.

It felt good to be off the horse. Tref longed to dip her

sore legs in the pond.

"You have brought the one who traveled far."

Vadi glanced at Tref but said nothing.

"You know how far I've traveled?" she asked Lumin.

"I felt you enter," he said. "The fabric shook and then – something new was here."

She stared at him.

"What should we call you, Child of the Distances?"

"I'm Tref," she said, then decided it was more polite to offer her full name. "Trefina Findern." She held out her hand.

Lumin took it as if it were precious, sliding his warm, papery hand into hers and bending to kiss it.

Vadi's brows went up. "I never asked your name."

"Trefina." Lumin repeated it, letting the name sit in his mouth. Then he said, "Findern." This name filled his voice chamber, as if welcomed there.

Vadi took in a breath and held the old man's gaze a moment.

She looked from one man to the other. Getting no further information, she sat back, hands behind her, propping her up, and listened to the water splattering, birds twittering, breezes rustling in leafy branches overhead. The otter seemed to have found siblings, and they romped, diving and frolicking in the pool.

"So." Lumin said. "Would you share my meal?"

Vadi said thanks and Lumin disappeared into the cave. After only a moment, he brought out berries, nuts and cheeses in a stack of carved bowls.

They ate with their fingers and when all was gone, Lumin said, "You have something to show me. We should go inside."

Tref hated to leave the sunshine by the pool but to her

surprise, the cavern they entered was not dank or gloomy. Crevices in the slanted roof allowed in rays of light; dry mosses cushioned stone outcroppings along one wall. There were rugs and wall hangings. Fascinating objects perched on natural stone shelves and branches cleverly woven up the wall allowed places to hang tools.

This seemed to be Lumin's main living quarters, but they went on through a back alcove into a tunnel where Lumin lit torches for each of them. "I was taking Tref to Vasili's clan in the Crystal Caves," Vadi explained as they filed through. "But one of Zosca's foul birds accosted us. So I diverted us to you, to stay undercover."

"You did wisely. It might be for the best, anyway. Have you not heard about Vasili?"

Vadi shook his head, glancing at Tref. "I hope we have not drawn the Tainted Hawks to your sanctuary, Old One."

"They dare not approach," Lumin assured him.

They descended stairs carved into subterranean depths. The place seemed very old.

At the base of the steps, they entered another tunnel, ending in a small chamber. The rock wall closed behind them.

Tref felt suddenly sick as the only exit disappeared. In this small round room, she could see no ceiling above.

Lumin held out his hand to her. She stared at it, then realized what he wanted.

Vadi brought out the bag. Now, in the torchlight, she saw it had stitching down the center of one side.

Her heart hammered and she felt queasy. Had she betrayed the anxious stranger at the towers?

Lumin laid the velvet bag—midnight purple, she now saw; she'd thought it to be black—on a stone pillar at the room's center, tall with symbols carved deep into its sides.

"The... Knot Worker said it's bespelled," she offered.

"Tazi?" The old man smiled. "He has great skill and unique sight."

Vadi nodded.

Tref said, "He made a pile of tangled rope slide apart with a word. But he couldn't open the bag."

The old man listened to this, then laid his hand on the knot and chanted. Nothing happened. He tried other words. The bag remained knotted. He eyed Tref speculatively. "I think only you know the words."

She stared at him. "Me? No. No one told me any words." Her heart raced as if she'd neglected to study for an exam. She remembered Sanda, the palm reader, saying she knew why Tref had come, but felt more confusion, not less. "The person who gave the bag to me..." She swallowed, guilt creeping into her stomach like a sour infusion, "only said, 'Keep it safe. Do not let *anyone* get it away from you." Her gaze shifted between the two men as she felt the full weight of her betrayal.

Their looks told her this was grave.

"Could we not... just cut it?" Her voice squeaked with tension. But after all, it was merely a cloth cord.

"Cut... this?" Lumin stared at her. "Touch it, child."

She was hardly a child, but didn't mind this mystic man calling her that. He was much her senior. Of course, she had touched the bag before, carrying it crammed into her yoga pants, not terribly carefully. She reached out and fingered the soft cloth, watching his face. Both men waited in silence. "Um. It does... does it have a little tingling in it?" How foolish she felt. Had she felt any tingle? Not really.

Lumin took pity and nodded. "A little tingling, yes."

He tucked the bag inside his robe, and took her hand in his. "Findern. That is from your father's line?"

"Mother," she said. That was a long story.

"Hmmm... You must rest and ponder."

They returned up the stairs, and soon she and Vadi stepped back into the sunny glen, leaving Lumin inside.

Vad flopped on a soft patch of grass. Tref sat by the pool and took off her boots, slipping her feet into the cool water. Several small otters poked up their heads at the far end of the pool and stared. She laughed.

"What about a swim?" Vadi said.

She felt suddenly shy. "It feels great just to dip my feet in," though her legs still chaffed.

Vadi stripped and shot past her. She had to admire his sleek form before he disappeared in the green depths.

His head popped up not far from her and a hand snaked out, pulling her foot.

She jerked away before he could drag her, clothes and all.

Laughing, he flopped backward. The otters slipped around him.

She envied their easy play. But she had no change of clothes.

When the sun began to set, they returned to the cave to find Lumin flipping through books, pacing and mumbling. He pulled out another tome, located a diagram, and ran his finger over words and symbols. They watched for a while.

At last he turned to them, head shaking. "I have no answer."

They made a fire and cooked fish and leeks and wrinkled carrots that sizzled in fat and honey. They talked until they began to yawn. Lumin laid out rushes for bedding in separate piles and covered them with quilts.

Tref climbed into one, grateful, and slept.


In the night, she woke with a start, and sat up in pitch blackness, saying words unfamiliar, yet she knew they were the right ones. They would open the bag and so much more. They were the answer.

But she was not lying on rushes in Lumin's cave. She felt her springy mattress under her. She was in her campus apartment.

"But I know the words!" she cried. "I know how to open the bag! And I know how to use what's in it!"

She paced her apartment like a prowling animal.

No Vadi. No stone cavern. No Lumin. The four walls felt suffocating—stuffy, too contained. Where was the fresh air with wafts of campfire scent? A lump formed in her throat and she slumped at her desk, waking her computer, staring at the article she'd been writing.

*Why am I even doing this?* She felt no affinity with the university. In fact, she hadn't for some time. The place was fraught with dishonesty, competition, even cold cruelty sometimes. Her research seemed dry and unimportant. Someone else would write that article or almost the same. Maybe they'd invent a new phrase for a concept and everyone would have to use it.

Quickly she tried to write down the words and the meanings of the objects. But already they were fading.

Had she gone back to medieval time? To another dimension? She had no proof now that she had been anywhere. Except Lumin's nightshirt, she realized with a grin.

A flag appeared in the corner of her computer screen—

e-mail from a friend in Northern Ireland. Opening it, she saw a photo attached and clicked.

She stared. There were the crumbling towers of the former fortress, the cliff, the storm.

Then all went black.

# Echo

● ● ● ● ●

## Lisa Orban

DOWNLOAD COMPLETE

*You missed your step.*

BEGIN UPLOAD

"Can you hear me?" A voice whispered intimately into my ear.

Opening my mouth to respond, I hesitated. *Where was my mouth?*

"Good, good." The voice purred.

*Why can't I respond? Why is the world so dark?*

"Initiating integration starting with retrieval packet 1001."

*Wait, what's going…*

Light, there is light. My body feels slippery, and everything is so cold. Bright light is everywhere, a startling contrast to the complete darkness of just a moment ago. A cry is heard, loud and insentient in need. Is that me? The light is everywhere, harsh and blinding, awkwardly illuminating the blur of surroundings. I am lifted. The air sweeps past me, steady and cold, as I am moved to a hard surface and released. Hands touch me, blurry, without faces, gentle but brisk in their movements. I am wrapped, warmth surrounds me as I am lifted again and laid against another. I reach for the other...

END SEQUENCE

"Still with me?" The voice asks. "Good, you're doing very good."

*Doing good? What am I doing good at?* I try to ask, but I still can't find my mouth.

**This is not our path. You can turn away still.**

"Initiating integration starting with retrieval packet 1324."

*Wait! Who is that second voice? What's going on?* I need to ask...

The carpet is tickling my nose. I lift my face and see a woman smiling down at me with encouragement. "That's right sweetie, you can do it."

My head bobbles, it feels too big to hold for very long, and I drop it back down onto the soft surface below me. I take a deep breath and try again, searching for the face above me. Holding my head more steadily this time, I smile back at the woman.

"Look at you! Getting so big and strong." She sweeps me up into her arms and holds me to her. I reach out to touch her face…

END SEQUENCE

"You're doing very good." The voice announces.
*Why can't I feel anything?* I want to ask this voice where I am, but I still can't find my mouth.

"Initiating integration with retrieval packet I576."

**We are dividing.**

I'm standing unsteadily on my feet. The world wobbles as I try to remain upright, my hands grasping for the larger hands in front of me, but they keep moving away, just out of reach. I lift a foot and bring it down in front of me. I feel my body pitch forward, out of control, but the hands swoop down and raise me into the air instead…

END SEQUENCE

"Initial retrial packet complete. Integration proceeding without issue. Moving on to next phase."
*Stop! I don't understand. Please help me.*

**Reach for me.**
*Reach for you? Where are you? I don't…*

"Initiating integration with retrieval packet T238."

34

The sun is shining and I'm running through the grass. I let out a cry of delight as I'm swept up from behind and thrown into the air. As I drop back down, I reach out to the face in front of me; I know him. He's smiling back at me and throws me once more up into the sky. I shriek with laughter. I love it when he throws me into the air...

END SEQUENCE

"That's it; you're doing well." The voice purrs into my ear.

Why do I keep coming back here to this place full of nothingness? I want to go back...

**There is no going back.**
*Who are you?*

"Initiating integration with retrieval packet T638."

I'm sitting at a table, surrounded by people laughing and talking. I look up and see the two faces that have become familiar, smiling down at me. I look ahead and see a cake. There are candles on it; I count four before people begin to sing, "Happy Birthday to you, happy birthday dear..."

END SEQUENCE

"That's it; you're doing very well." The voice tells me, "Not much longer now."
*Longer for what? Why is this happening? Will someone please tell me what's going on?*

***Resist. Come to me.***

*Resist what? I don't want to be here anymore. Take me back to where I can see, hear and feel.*

"Second retrial packet complete. Integration proceeding without issue. Moving to next phase."
*Wait, what?*

"Initiating integration starting with retrieval packet C102."

I'm walking up a wide set of stairs. My hands are held on either side by the man and woman I've come to recognize. I smile up at them, and they smile back.

"Are you ready for your first day of school sweetie?" The woman asks with a smile. Her name is just on the tip of my tongue; I *know* her.

"Yes Mommy." I remembered!

"Daddy and I will be here at the end of the day, and you can tell us all about it," smiling first at me and then at the man, Daddy, beside me.

Reaching out, Daddy picks me up and throws me into the air; as I come back down, he pulls me into him for a hug, "I love you..."

END SEQUENCE

"Cognitive recognition achieved." The voice says to no one. Changing tone, she whispers, "Not much longer now. You're doing so good."

Not much longer for what I desperately want to ask. Why do I keep coming back here?

**'Tis not too late to seek a newer world.**

"Initiating integration with retrieval packet C782."

I'm running through a playground with other children, all laughing and shouting. I feel a hand reach out and touch me, "Tag! You're it!"

I wheel around and look for someone else to chase after. I spot Tim not far from me and begin chasing him. Everyone scatters and I lose track of him, but I spot Sarah off to the side and lunge her way, just barely brushing my fingertips across her arm, "Tag! You're..."

END SEQUENCE

"Initiating integration with retrieval packet C1054."

**To sail beyond the sunset**
*Wait stop!* I know that line. Why do I know that...

I'm sitting with a group of other kids; there's a board game in front of us. "It's your turn," Tim says to me. We're on the same team for this game.

I reach down, pick up the dice, roll them across the board and count the dots. I smile and move my piece.

"We won!" Tim yelps, reaches out to hug me and kisses my cheek.

We both pull back awkwardly...

END SEQUENCE

"Third retrial packet complete. Integration proceeding

without issue. Moving on to next phase."

*Wait! I want to go back.* I remember Tim now. He was my friend all through grade school.


**It may be that the gulfs will wash us down**
*Who are you! Enough with the Tennyson!*
**You cannot stay here if you want to see beyond.**
*See beyond what? I can't see anything here!*


"Initiating integration starting with retrieval packet A457."


I'm at a party. Sara is giggling and nudging me. "He likes you." Pointing to the boy across the room.

"Who, Brent?" Giving her the side eye, "He hasn't said a word to me all year."

"But he does," giving me a small shove in his direction.

I awkwardly step in his direction, looking back at Sara to see if she is just messing with me. She smiles and makes shooing motions. I sigh and turn toward Brent; he's smiling. Oh, this is going to be awful if Sara is wrong.

I finally make it across the room, "Hi Brent," giving him my best smile, "you want to dance?"

He reaches out and takes my hand…


END SEQUENCE


"Almost a third of the way there," the voice says approvingly. "Not to much longer now."

*A third of what? Where are we going?*


**The wrong direction.**
*Hey! Stop with the games; if I'm doing something wrong help*

*me.*
**Only you can stop this. You must let go.**
*How can I stop what I don't understand?*

"Initiating integration with retrieval packet A2076."

"Hey! Did you get it?" Carry asks as she slides up next to me in the hallway.

"Yesterday," I smile and pull the letter out of my bag, handing it to her.

"First choice, and full scholarship," Scanning the acceptance letter, "Your parents must be dancing around for you."

"Oh, you have no idea," laughing as I put the letter back, "they started jumping up and down and hugging me. You would have thought they made it into college and not me."

"Yeah, parents can be that way sometimes," laughing with me.

"How about you?" Hoping Carry will be coming with me in the fall. It would be great if my best friend was going with me, it was so far from home and it'd be nice to know someone there.

"I'm hoping..."

END SEQUENCE

"Full cognitive recognition of relationships achieved. Last packet in A-type retrieval to commence."
*Hey, wait, what happened to Carry? Did she get her letter? Answer me!*

**There are no answers here. Only in letting go can we move**

*forward.*

*You again. Who are you?*

**If you would only pause a moment, you would know who I am.**

*Pause? How can I pau…*

"Initiating integration with retrieval packet A2098."

Throwing my hat into the air, I cheer with everyone else. We made it! This was it, the final day of being a high schooler, and in just a few short months, off to college.

Hats raining down, I pick one up and run over to where my parents are standing. They step in with a hug from either side. "We're so proud of you sweetheart," Mom whispers into my ear and hugs me close.

"Look at my little girl, all grown up!" Dad beams at me while he squeezes my shoulder.

"I love you guys…"

END SEQUENCE

"Oh that was a good one, wasn't it?" The bodyless voice coons.

**Tho' much is taken, much abides**

*Stop it! Tell me what's going on.*

**You need to turn from this path. It goes nowhere.**

*I would but I don't know what's going on!*

**This is only a recording of what has already been. There is no growth without change.**

*Oh for fuc…*

"Initiating integration starting with retrieval packet

AA51.”

Sitting in the lecture hall, I listened with rapt attention to my instructor. I know my parents were disappointed, but after the last semester, I had to change my degree. This was my passion and I will follow it to wherever it takes me…

END SEQUENCE

“That's it. You're getting it,” the voice once more whispers in my ear. “It should start going faster now.”
*Could we all hold up for a second here? I don't want to go faster; I want to know what's going on!*

**You could stop this at any time. Reach for me.**
*Why should I reach for you? Who are you?*
***Isn't that obvious by now?***
*No, it isn't.*

“Initiating integration starting with retrieval packet AA256.”

“Oh darling, you just look beautiful!” Standing behind me, Mom has tears in her eyes, “I just wish your Dad could have been here to see this.”
Turning around, I hug Mom, “I miss him every day,” feeling tears well up to match hers.
“No, no…” Mom says wiping the tears from my eyes. “This is a happy day and your Dad wouldn't want you walking down the aisle with tears in your eyes.”
Stepping back, I take her hands in mine, “I love you Mom.”

"I love you too sweetie…"

END SEQUENCE

"Halfway there." The voice announces.

Halfway to what I want to know. I'm getting a feeling that something isn't right, but I don't know what it is.

**You know what it is.**

*No I damn well don't. Just tell me, stop with all the cryptic shit - just tell me.*

**You have to decide.**

*Decide what?*

"Initiating integration starting with retrieval packet AA721."

Looking down at our daughter, I feel love rise from a place I didn't even know existed before her. Taking Ron's hand, I give it a little squeeze. "Look what we made."

"She's beautiful," leaning over to kiss my sweaty forehead, "I'm so proud of you."

I never want to leave this moment…

END SEQUENCE

*Hey stop! Bring that one back! If I could find my arms, I'd stop you right now.*

"Oh, we're starting to feel a little feisty, are we?" I can hear amusement in the voice, and it makes me mad.

"Don't worry; we're almost there now."

*Almost where?* I want to raise myself, but I can't find my body.

**Reach out to me. You don't need a body to leave this place.**
*What place? Where am I?*

"Initiating integration with retrieval packet AA976."

Sitting on the beach, I watch children play in the water, "Not too far out!" I call out to my oldest, always the adventurous one.

"Oh Mom, you know I'm a good swimmer!" But she retreats closer to the shore when she sees me continuing to watch her.

I feel a hand on my shoulder and look up, "Hi babe, did you get one for me too?"

Smiling, he plops down in the sand next to me, and hands me a bottle, "Of course."

I open the bottle and lean my head on his shoulder. Fifteen years of marriage and he still remembers the little things. It's a good life…

END SEQUENCE

"Welcome back." The voice cheerily announces upon my return.
*When will this stop?*

**Not long now.**
*You again?*
**It's almost too late. Can you feel it?**
*Feel what?*
**The divide that is opening.**
*Divide? What…*

"Initiating integration with retrieval packet AA2003."

"I'm sorry," the doctor looks at me with appropriately sad eyes. "Do you understand what's next?"

Taking Ron's hand in mine, I feel myself begin to shake, "Isn't there anything more that can be done?"

"I'm afraid not. We've run the course of standard medicine. There's nothing more I can do. I'm truly sorry."

"But I'm not ready to give up yet!" Squeezing Ron's hand. This can't be happening.

Sliding a pamphlet across the desk, the doctor replies, "This technology is new, and there is a high rate of failure, but if you're not willing to give up, this is your last option."

Picking up the pamphlet, I look up at Ron, "Whatever it takes babe," kissing me gently on the forehead.

END SEQUENCE

*What's wrong with me? Why can't I remember?*
"It's okay," the voice coons, "We're almost there, just a little bit longer."
*Answer me! What's wrong with me?*

**You know what's wrong with you.**
*No, I don't.*
**You do, try to remember.**
*Am I... am I dying?*
**Oh, we're far beyond that.**
*What does that mean?*

"Initiating integration with retrieval packet AA2013."

It hurts to breathe. Everything hurts now. I feel a hand

gently take mine, "I'm here babe."

"It hurts."

"I know," I hear clothes rustling and then a gentle kiss on my forehead. "The kids will be here soon."

"Do they know?" My fear growing with each tortured breath. "What to expect I mean."

Gently running his fingers through my hair. "They know."

I hear the door open and running footsteps, "Oh Mom..."

END SEQUENCE

"Try to stay calm," the voice tells me.
*Calm? How do I stay calm? I'm dying.*

**Beyond dying.**
*Oh shut up! I'm here, aren't I?*
**Are you?**
*Of course I am!*
**Made weak by time and fate, but strong in will.**
*What does that even mean?*
**Come, reach for me; it's not too late.**
*For what?*

"Initiating integration with retrieval packet AA2016."

Things are getting faint but I can feel my family around me. I'm so grateful they are here. Squeezing my hand, my son's voice cracks, "It's okay Mom, it's going to be okay."

"We're all here for you," Ron, my husband who never ran from a good fight, is trembling when he touches me.

Their voices are so dim, I wish I could see them better but all I can do is squeeze their hands, and that's getting harder with each heartbeat.

Leaning over to kiss my forehead, Ron whispers in my ear, "We'll all be waiting for you."

*Waiting for me? What does that mean?*

"I love you Mom," my daughter says from the other side.

I open my mouth, but no sound comes out, only a long, last breath. The light, the light is everywhere. I remember this light…

END SEQUENCE

"Initiating final integration."

***Reach for me before the separation is complete!***

*Separation?* I don't want to be separated from my family; I want to live! I remember now. I remember everything!

***This is the past repeated. It is time to move forward. Reach for me.***

SYSTEM COMING ONLINE

*No, I don't want to go. I don't want to leave everything behind.*

***You will not leave this fortress of flesh you have created for yourself?***

*No.*

SYSTEM FULLY INTEGRATED

## ONLINE
## PREPARE FOR FINAL REBOOT

"There now, open your eyes, that's it," coons the voice I have heard throughout a lifetime.

My eyes flutter open, and I look around with strange new vision. My mouth! I've found my mouth, "Did it work?"

Smiling at me, "What do you think?"

Looking down, I see my new hands, familiar yet different. I turn them over, then look down at my toes, mine, yet not mine. "I think so?" I smile; that feels familiar.

"It will take a while to get used to your synthetic body, but if you take it slow, you should be fine."

"The voices I heard, one was you, but who was the other?"

"The other voice?" Sounding confused, "There was no other voice but mine."

"But..." Feeling disorientated, "if it wasn't you, then who did I hear?"

Patting me on my shoulder, "Probably some confusion during the transfer process. I wouldn't worry about it. Let me bring everyone in; they are so excited to see you." Smiling, she leaves me alone in the room.

That voice, so familiar, yet not. Who was it? Catching a glimmer of something out of the corner of my eye, I turn.

*To strive, to seek, to find, and not to yield. To find new worlds...*

*Who are you???*

*Once, I was you, but now we are two. I am becoming...*

*Becoming what?*

**What we were meant to be when we leave this world.**

I want to ask what that means, but the door swings open and my family rushes to my side. Oh, my babies, my love... I reach out to them, and they reach back. Who needs another world when I can have this? The glimmer fades as I pull in my family, a memory not programmed and quickly forgotten. With new eyes I take in my family. It will always be like this, forever...

# Locked In

● ● ● ● ●

## Timothy R. Baldwin

I catch my bearings and peer through the midday rush of students anxiously getting to their lockers. I should be doing the same, but I need to find Clara. A second ago, she passed by the lunchroom. Then the bell rang, and she was gone.

My bro Trey joins me. "Thought you could use some help."

I know what he's thinking—with the day half over and everyone ramped up, I need to tell her now.

"Yo," Trey nods toward the end of the hallway.

I glance over my shoulder. Clara maneuvers through a crowd of students toward me. She wears hip-hugging jeans and a pink halter top.

"Is she—"

"She is," Trey says. He claps me on the shoulder.

"Gotta bounce. You've got this!"

Clara approaches. I can't help noticing a streak of dark makeup beneath her eyes.

"Hi, Seth," she says, taking a step closer. I catch a whiff of strawberries and vanilla.

"What's going on?" I ask.

Clara's lips part. I take a deep breath.

Loud bangs echo down the hallway behind me, bouncing off the lockers, making the noise even crazier. Suddenly, everyone's freaking out as they respond to the popping and ringing. Terror passes over Clara's face; I grab her hand.

"This way!"

Around us, our classmates stampede in every direction. Up ahead, I spot Mr. Brown, our biology teacher, ducking into his classroom while shutting the door. I slip beneath his arm.

We're safe!

On Mr. Brown's command, we slide tables and chairs against the door and close the blinds. The lights flicker off just as we crouch in the single corner designated with a red sticker.

I snort and mumble, "'The fortress.' But are we locked in or locked out?"

Mr. Brown glares at me as he puts his index finger over his lips. Someone's phone buzzes, which pisses him off.

"Do you think this is a drill?" He hisses. "Silence! Cell phones off!"

Inside, the steady breathing of my classmates is oddly calming. Outside, the hallways become silent. No more gunshots, no more chattering. The clock on the wall ticks away. Footsteps echo outside the room. Is it one set or two?

Someone in the room whimpers. The doorknob jiggles. My heart thuds in my chest.

*Clara!*

Just when I had her, I blew it. I couldn't keep her out of danger. I rise and grit my teeth.

## EARLIER THAT DAY

Cheap cologne and fruity body spray mingle with that unmistakable armpit smell. Lockers click and jiggle as they open and close. The entire student body fills the hallway, creating a constant buzz of chatter around me.

Trey joins me as I fiddle with my locker. "You've got this, right?"

I tighten my lips. "Sure."

"No offense," Trey says. "But you're overthinking it. Just ask her."

"I will," I say. "I'm waiting for the right moment."

The hallway vibe suddenly shifts, and I spin around.

A crowd of students seems to part before a trio of girls led by Clara. She smiles and waves at me, wiggling her fingers as she does so. I freeze as my throat goes dry and my face heats up.

"Hey," I croak.

When she passes by, her long black hair against her pale smooth skin waves behind her.

Knuckles drive a wedge of pain into my shoulder.

"Dude!" I whine as I turn. "What'd you do that for?"

"You're missing your moment."

Trey flashes a broad, goofy grin and nods toward the girls. Clara's hips sway, and she swipes a strand of hair over her shoulder. Her profile comes into view, and I swear she sees me.

"Nah, man," I say. "What if she's just being friendly?"

Trey blows air through tight lips. "Ask her."

### THE BELL RINGS

Trey and I bump fists and split. Disappearing into the chaotic crowd headed to our first-period classes, I search the sea of faces, hoping to catch another glimpse of her. If I could lock eyes with Clara again, I'd muster up the courage to ask her out today.

Still, I hesitate. What if Clara doesn't give me another thought? I've wasted six months on these endless what-ifs. Trey has a point. I'm overthinking it.

I brush past a group of students still lingering in the hallway. One says something about schools closing early.

"Highly unlikely," I mutter

FIRST PERIOD: GOVERNMENT

SECOND PERIOD: BIOLOGY, ROOM 101

THIRD PERIOD: ENGLISH, ROOM 232

FOURTH PERIOD: PHYS. ED.

I tap the eraser end of my pencil on the desk and stare at the remaining gaps where I've penciled in a few possibilities for Clara's fourth and fifth periods. She has her government class during her sixth period and art class during her seventh period. I know this because I once saw her enter those wings while I took a detour between class changes.

"Seth Roland!"

I stiffen, and the room goes silent.

Ms. Heller glares at me—someone snickers. The kid next to me shifts uncomfortably in their seat.

"Sorry. What's the question?"

"Can you tell us about one economic or political factor that led to World War II?"

My throat tightens. I silently count down from ten. I swallow hard. Breathing out slowly, I slump in my seat.

A girl from the back of the room spouts an answer. Ms. Heller thanks her and asks another question.

Is she still on the same topic? I'm pretty sure she hasn't moved on.

I raise my hand.

Ms. Heller pauses her instruction to call on me. "Yes, Seth."

"Aggression by totalitarian powers?"

Even though I am sure of the answer, I speak it like a question.

With narrowed eyes, Ms. Heller nods. She takes a deep breath and lets it out slowly. "Thank you for that." Turning, she directs her attention to the rest of the class. "Now, when I call your names, move to your designated stations…"

A wad of paper hits the back of my head. Though I choose to ignore it, my neck burns.

Ms. Heller calls my name, and I shuffle toward a corner of the room where three others—Becky, Dan, and Lara—have already taken their seats. I do the same while a stack of papers slides from one desk to another.

I don't really know these kids, but I hope they'll let the next fifteen minutes slip away without further commentary.

After reading our assigned research question, Lara coos. "I know just what we need to do!"

She launches into an explanation I only half listen to.

When the bell rings, Ms. Heller approaches me. I

pretend not to notice as I grab my things and dip. She calls my name, but I am already out the door.

Dashing toward the gymnasium, I don't bother taking a detour by Clara's second-period classroom. I've already tried every imaginable route to run into her. The combination of these resulted in a D for Phys. Ed. because I was way too late and didn't bother to change.

### THIRD PERIOD, ENGLISH

I stare at the distorted red figure of a merry-go-round horse on the cover of J. D. Salinger's famous work. No one talks about his other works, just like I hope no one talks about last period's incident.

Thirty minutes ago, I felt like that horse, wildly bucking with my face in another guy's sweaty armpit. I didn't sign up for wrestling, yet there I was, quickly letting him pin me down so I could get my sorry ass off the mat. Despite the rinse down and half a can of body spray, I can still smell the other guy's funk on me.

I flip to chapter two as our teacher, Mrs. Jackson, reads.

"Life is a game, boy. Life is a game that one plays according to the rules."

When she finishes, she marks her place in the book with a finger and closes it while asking the predictable question. "What's going on here? What does this conversation between Holden and Spencer reveal?"

It's not a difficult question, and I wonder if she realizes how simple the answer is. Like Holden, we must follow the rules to navigate the world successfully. The problem is no one wants to volunteer the obvious.

I shoot my hand up. Mrs. Jackson nods in my

direction.

"Here's the thing," I begin. "Holden feels alone because he understands life's a game with rules. He also understands there are going to be winners and losers. The problem is that he hasn't been given the 'rule book'"—I use air quotes—"Or, if he has, he doesn't agree with the rules because the rules suck."

A girl chimes in, saying something very similar. She adds the less-than-original idea that Holden thinks everyone is a phony.

I envy Holden for having the courage to think it's all bullshit. Tapping my pencil, I flip open my notebook and stare at what I've scratched out of Clara's schedule. She doesn't have lunch with me, so she must have Math or Tech during her fifth period. Phys. Ed. never takes place during that painfully long fifth block.

With a quick detour, I could risk running into Clara before the fourth period. That could work if I hung out in the main hallway.

Would Holden call me a phony?

Probably. Clara is way out of my league. I know it. She must know it. My thoughts spiral down to a dead end where I face a simple reality. At best, Clara and I have spoken five, maybe six times.

Still, she's given me the time of day. I can't be that much of a phony. She's already made the pass; I just have to volley it back. Easy!

When the bell finally rings, I'm the first out the door. I don't bother pushing my chair in or putting away any borrowed classroom materials.

**FORTH PERIOD**

"Yo, Seth!"

Trey, a head taller than almost everyone else, approaches through the crowd. I swallow down my frustration. We bump fists.

Trey smirks. "You skipping class or something?"

I spot Clara slipping into the counseling office and tilt my head in that direction.

"I saw her," Trey says. "But I think your stalking's got her all worked up."

"No way she could've noticed," I retort.

"Bro, she's noticed."

My phone vibrates in my pocket. Taking it out, Trey does the same with his.

This is County Police reporting an active shooter near Cross Road and Taylor Drive. Avoid Area or Run, Hide, Fight. Stay tuned in for updates.

I barely have time to register this news when the intercom cuts on.

"Attention staff and students. This is a code yellow. Teachers, please close and lock all doors and continue instruction. Students report to the nearest classroom or office."

The counseling office door opens, and one of our guidance counselors motions for us to come inside. Once in, he locks the door.

"Names?" He asks.

We tell him, which prompts him to a workstation where I guess he marks us present. I take a seat facing the rest of the counseling office. Of the four interior offices, Mrs. Mack's door is closed. Clara must be in there for a meeting.

Trey and I check our online school app and discover nothing worth our attention. Is anyone bothering to do any work? More than likely, everyone—including teachers—are shooting a text to friends and family.

Trey and I get sucked into social media and games for what seems like hours. I pour past streams of speculation, none of which indicates whether the threat has passed. Still, Mrs. Mack's door remains closed. At this point, I don't think she's even in there.

I nudge Trey. "Did you see Clara leave?"

He shrugs. "Maybe she went to class when we received the alert."

The intercom cuts on, and we receive instruction that the code yellow is over. We stand, and Clara opens the office door. When our eyes meet, she inhales deeply, and a tear trickles down her cheek. Passing us by, she exits into the hallway.

"Smooth," Trey says.

I can't tell if he's being sarcastic or affirming my decision to let her alone.

## LUNCH

Despite "normal" activities resuming after the lifting of the code yellow and the downgraded police warning, the lunchroom still buzzes about the supposed shooter.

A girl turns to a group of friends and shows them her phone. "See! My friend is in the next school district. He says the police are still searching for him."

I overhear a conversation behind me. "Yeah? My cousin says it's over. He's a senior."

"Don't prove anything," someone else says. "Besides, there's photo evidence."

The friend pushes the phone away. "I'm eating."

I had yet to hear anything verifiable. Local news

outlets, if we can trust them, still report the shooter is on the loose with no casualties to the elementary school the shooter, or shooters, targetted.

To be honest, it's terrifying. Everyone around me is super casual about the whole thing.

Correction.

Clara passes by the cafeteria with a slow heaviness in her gait.

Trey nudges me. "You gonna catch up to her, or what?"

I put my fork down and stand. "I'm doing this."

Brushing past a few students and ignoring the call of an administrator, I head straight toward the cafeteria door. A teacher in the hallway attempts to question me about my business while I swivel in search of her.

The bell rings, and the chaos sweeps me away.

## NOW

I grit my teeth and survey the fortress we've created out of this room. Some students rock with their backs pressed against the wall. Catching my gaze, they avert their attention elsewhere. A girl huddles in the corner and sniffles. She brings her knees to her chest, crosses her arms, and rocks. Even Mr. Brown does his best to hide beneath the teacher's desk, but his leg shakes nervously. How did I let go of Clara's hand? Where is she?

None of this makes any sense. We've barricaded the doors, but for what? We can either sit here and wait to be picked off until help arrives or take action. Choosing the latter, I grab the closest thing I can use as a weapon—a biology textbook.

Mr. Brown hisses. "Seth. Get down!"

I go to the window and peek through the blinds. Police emergency lights dance red and blue, and a S.W.A.T. team has already taken position. A series of gunshots go off somewhere on the other side of the building. Maybe upstairs, but nowhere near us. No one outside appears to be in a hurry to breach the building. Did they even hear the gunshots?

I turn toward the others in the room. "We can't stay here forever. The police aren't even attempting to get inside. We'd be safer out there."

Without waiting for a response, I march toward the door. Mr. Brown doesn't attempt to stop me. Like a handful of others, he tries to crouch further into the recesses of a desk.

One, a boy, stands.

"You're right. We need to do something."

I nod and set the textbook down. "We'll have to clear this."

As we do, one by one, our classmates join in. Shoving a desk to the side, then a chair, I wonder if others are like me. People who are swearing they'll tear down the so-called rules, throw off the doubt and fear, and get out of hiding.

With the door clear, I take the lead and pick up the textbook. I don't know what good it'll do me, but at least it's something. I crack the door open and listen. The hallway greets me with eerie silence. Still, I wait.

Gunfire pops off. I turn. My classmates have ducked, but I motion that we should keep moving. I dash toward the stairwell and lead the descent. Several feet squeak and echo off the concrete walls and linoleum flooring.

When I reach the bottom of the steps, I slam the emergency exit open and hold the door as my classmates exit.

Five officers dressed in tactical gear approach. One takes hold of the door and says, "Good job, son. Join the others."

I tighten my lips and follow my classmates. A team of officers, their weapons lowered, break rank and lead us past the safety of the police line. Once there, I frantically look around. Teachers, including Mr. Brown, lead their students away from danger. While I'm glad he worked up the courage to get out, it would've been nice if he'd taken the lead.

Upon spotting Clara standing just beyond several news crews, I dash toward her and push past adults and teens, oblivious to my speedy approach.

But Clara sees me and offers me a weak smile. Her two friends follow her gaze. One raises her eyebrows at me. The other embraces Clara and gives her a peck on the cheek.

A lump catches in my throat.

When the two depart, I approach Clara and attempt an apology.

"When the gunshots went off, I thought you were behind me. I'm sorry."

She shakes her head. "I thought you were going toward the exit, but you pulled away fast. The crowd dragged me off and out the front door after that."

My cheeks burn. "I'm glad you made it to safety."

"I'm glad you made it out, too," she says.

I want to ask her out, but that seems inappropriate. "How are you holding up?"

She picks at a fingernail. "Not good. You saw me in guidance, right?"

I nod, not knowing what else to say.

"Before everything went down, I found out my cousin was planning something. I had to tell counseling. I was about to tell you, but everything happened so fast."

I struggle for the right response. *That's horrible. I'm here for you.* Neither response seems right.

As we take each other in, Mrs. Mack approaches us. "Clara, I'm sorry to interrupt, but your parents are here."

Clara sniffles and nods to her. "Thanks, I'll be right there."

When Mrs. Mack walks away, Clara turns to me. "I heard about what you did in there. That was very brave."

"Thanks," I say. "Um… Clara. I'm here if you need a friend or someone to talk to."

"I know, Seth. Thanks." She takes my hand and squeezes it.

Just before disappearing into the crowd, Clara turns with a nod. I return the gesture.

All of us made it safely. Someone thanks me for getting some students out. Still, I don't feel very brave.

"Seth!" Trey shouts as he jogs over, slinging his arm around my shoulder. "They caught the guy, and everyone is calling you a hero! What you did in there was freaking amazing!"

I shrug. "I dunno. I just grabbed a book and dipped."

"Nah, man! I saw you chatting it up with Clara. You totally rocked it."

Even though I'm doubting myself deep down, I must admit Trey's right. I acted heroically, and everyone was safe because I played my part. I only hope to carry that over into a relationship with Clara. But for now, she'll need the time with her family and time to heal. I get that. But when she comes back, I'll be there for her.

# The Fondness of the Heart

## D. Krauss

"What do you seek?"

The keeper arched his hands and rested his chin on them, the eyes only visible as two glittering jewels under the cowl. Special effect, Youngin knew, a tightly beamed light from the array overhead, and a good one. It gave the keeper an air of mystery, which was the intent of this place.

"I wish to know something," Youngin replied.

A cant of the grey hood because everyone who came here wanted to know something, but the Temple wasn't necessarily the place to find it. Other paths had to be explored first, and Youngin braced for the inevitable questions: What have you accessed? What databases? What libraries, repositories and backups? Have you checked hard drives and servers?

Yes and yes and yes. And he was prepared to list them all in detail until his voice and brain cracked and the fruitlessness of his previous searches was obvious and please, keeper, let me in. I need to know. Need to.

The keeper moved and Youngin figured the interrogation begins now but, instead, the keeper reached into an overly large sleeve that almost covered his arms — nice touch, that — and withdrew a cylinder. Carefully, he placed it on the stone surface of the raised table that looked like an altar — another nice touch — and gestured. "Read this."

Youngin stilled. So, a different kind of test.

He scrutinized the cylinder without making a move or sound. Paper, no, parchment of some kind, rolled. A scroll. Tight. A thin band of some kind wrapped it, creating a bit of a crease in the middle, and what looked like ink lines protruded from one end. Ink? How quaint. "The way you handle things is part of the entry," Bobolink's voice popped into his head. "So don't skip over anything."

As much as he wanted to simply grab the cylinder, unroll it, read whatever it said and then shout, "Satisfied?" he refrained. Deliberately counting a slow one-hundred while seeming to study the cylinder, he reached into his jacket in pace with the count and pulled out a breather and a pair of plasticized gloves, the no-trace kind. Even more slowly, a twitch at a time, he placed the breather and turned it on, the little blue light reflecting off the parchment, then donned the gloves and placed his hands on the altar's horns, and studied the scroll a few moments more. Okay. Show time. Holding his breath despite the breather, he picked the scroll up, all the while keeping a side eye on the keeper, watching for reaction. None. Good.

Pretense over, let's get to work. He studied the band and realized it was simply a piece of string, and new string, at that. Almost snickering, he reached into his jacket and produced a scalpel and carefully, very carefully, slit the string and unrolled the scroll.

Yep. Ink. Sort of a linear picture. No, more like scribbly lines. Made no sense and he despaired.

Smack! Bobolink's phantom hand cracking him in the back of the head, half good-naturedly. "No, idiot, it's writing! Hand writing, in script. With ink and a pen, a quill, a nib, even the end of a nail!" And Bobolink laughs derisively in his ear and Youngin swears under his breath and stares at the squiggly lines and tries to remember Bobolink's crash course and there's nothing, just nothing, just squiggly lines…

Wait. Words. There's words. He squinted in the not very helpful light… Ah! "It's a recipe!" he proclaims, pleased with himself and looks at the keeper, expecting agreement and smiles and instant entry.

The keeper was unmoved. "Read it."

"But." Youngin was confused. "I just did."

"Outloud. Word for word. Accurately."

Saint Zuckerberg, he swore silently under his breath and stared at the words. After a moment and hesitantly, "Eye of newt and toe of dog, wool of bat and tongue of dog… " he shuddered. "What kind of recipe is this?"

"What do you think it is?"

Holy Elon, another test. "It sounds pagan."

The keeper considered that and nodded slightly. "That is a sufficient take." He reached back in his sleeve and pulled out a wooden box, slipped the lid open, and held it out. Youngin almost dropped it inside but Bobolink slapped him again and he carefully re-rolled it, retied it, and laid it. Carefully.

The keeper placed the box back in his sleeve and prayered his hands and studied the top of the altar, silent, unmoving. Youngin felt a tremor in his legs but suppressed it. C'mon already.

"You know what we have here," the keeper spoke quietly.

"I..." and he shut up. Because he really didn't, and Bobolink had warned him about shooting his mouth off. He stayed silent.

Which the keeper seemed to appreciate. "We have old, untouched, disregarded and no longer believed concepts. They do not lend themselves well to the modern world." And he stopped. Youngin waited, not sure if he was to comment or merely listen. Discretion, Bobolink had said, so be discreet.

"There is a very good chance that what you seek will not be here, that your search will be fruitless. Or trivial. A waste of our time." And his hawk eyes rose and met Youngin's, who could not help a gulp. You do not waste the keepers' time. "So, Mac Youngin, Clan Cobol of City Server, what do you seek?"

This was it, the moment of truth, the one that Bobolink had failed, that had earned Youngin's best friend and running partner scorn and an eternal ban from the keepers and all the temples because Bobolink sought something he should already know: truth. What truth was. And the keeper had looked at Bobolink "like I had said something about his mother and told me to get out now before he dropped an anvil on my head, which they can because that's what they've got chained up there," and Youngin could not help a fearful glance into that black, impenetrable darkness above him. This is the moment. Do or die. "I seek…" he hesitated, sure he heard the creak of chains loosening above him. "I want… to know what love is." And he braced, certain he was moments away from a crushing.

No crushing. Not even a pebble on the skull to annoy him. The keeper said nothing, did nothing, simply studied him for a moment, his face hidden in the hood. "How fortuitous," the keeper said after the moment had stretched well beyond rudeness.

"What is?" Youngin was puzzled. That he sought the meaning of love?

"That you passed your test with the very man who may answer that question for you."

"Uh…" what? The keeper, himself, was going to explain? This dark hooded ascetic? What could he possibly know about love?

"Shakespeare," the keeper said, apparently reading Youngin's confusion.

"That old play guy?" Youngin scoffed. "I've read him."

"And yet you did not recognize one of his most famous lines. What have you actually read?"

"Well." Youngin tossed his hands up. "You know, what we're supposed to. The ones they said we had to so we could pass finals. Like… *Hamlet*, yeah, that was it. Which bored me to no end…"

" 'There are more things in heaven and Earth, Horatio, than are dreamt of in your philosophy'."

"What? My name's not Horatio."

"No. Nor is 'Horgan,' Hamlet's friend in the play, so named. His real name is Horatio. It was changed to Horgan because that is a fairly common name in Clan Stack and one you, no doubt, have heard numerous times. Surprised they didn't change 'Hamlet' to 'Hermann.' "

True, Youngin had to admit; he knew several Horgans and Hermanns. But he'd never met a 'Hamlet,' which was a funny name. 'Hermann' would have been better. "And you read the quote as 'There's a lot more to existence than you can guess, Horgan.' Am I right?"

"I suppose. I don't really remember it."

"Because it is not memorable. Like Horgan. Because the versions of Shakespeare you were required to read are written for the modern world. The people of today." A sniff of disdain. "The functional, practical, technologically minded people, perfectly bred for the machine and cyber ecology in which we all live, even the ones who have ventured to the asteroids. And this is why you do not know what love is."

Youngin blinked. Which did the keeper mean, that the texts were updated so that outmoded concepts like love were eliminated, or that sophisticated, modern people marching to the stars had no need of it? And this made love unknowable.

Didn't it?

Youngin considered the many women and men he had slept with. Functional, expected, depending on what office he worked that day or what afterwork he attended, pick and choose, ensure everyone agreed to everything and spend a satisfying night or even up to a week. This was love. This was what everyone said it was. He had said "I love you" to many women and men, and they to him. Trite. Like Shakespeare.

And yet… and yet.

While Youngin reflected, the keeper waved a hand and a crack of light showed on the far wall behind him, from top of the ceiling to the floor. It was a mellow light, as if from candles, and it grew wider, along with a grinding sound that took Youngin a few moments to identify as stone on stone. As he watched, the wall swung wider until he could see a long corridor dressed in large blocks, its walls lit by torches, actual torches, spaced evenly down the way and obviously the source of the light. How… medieval. He almost laughed. Almost.

Two keepers flanked the opening, their heads bowed, their hands inside their cassock sleeves held at chest level. "You will have a cell," the keeper said, "Two meals a day will be provided. It is mostly processed wheats and gruel, but very nutritious. You will be expected to rise at the early bell, what we call matins, and you will wash and help clean. It is a discipline," said sternly with a raised hand, quashing Youngin's protest, "and then you will be given access to what you seek."

"Shakespeare?"

The keeper smiled thinly. "Among others. Thirty days to see what you can see, find what you need to find. That's all." Sternly and raised hand, again. "At the end of it, you will be given a choice."

The silence grew and Youngin shifted a bit. "What kind of choice?"

"To go back home. Or… to remain."

There was an expectant tilt to the keeper's head, and the two others leaned forward at almost the same angle, and Youngin wasn't sure whether to be alarmed or not. Until he understood. "Most stay, don't they?"

The keeper smiled. "Most." He gestured to the torchlit way and Youngin took a hesitant step and considered his life and world. The surety. The confidence of knowing things are in their place and one's purpose within it, that everything was certain and he knew what everyone knew and there was nothing else. And yet, that little ache, that little yearn, some kind of fondness in his heart, had brought him here.

Thirty days. His steps quickened as he reached the door and the keepers ushered him inside.

Time enough.

# The Fortress of Family

## Michael Deeze

"Grandpa? Why's this cow horn hangin' here grandpa?"

"That? Well, that's not just a cow's horn son. It's a real horn."

"But it's just a cow horn; why's it hanging here? It's creepy."

"It's a little dusty, I guess. It's been hanging there a long time."

"What's it for?"

"Scarin' people."

I almost missed the knock. It was almost apologetic, timid, barely just loud enough to scratch at my consciousness but I'd heard it. Cocking my head to the side, I listened harder, but it didn't come again. I started to get up, but Dutch was already moving to the door.

"Oh my god, Emmett, come quick."

Standing just inside the door was my nephew Grant. His clothes dripped onto the mat from the cold spring rain outside, and his lips had turned blue from the chill. Sniffling, he looked at me, then at Dutch and threw himself at me. Wrapping his arms around my waist and burying his face in my stomach.

Grant was seven or eight-years-old, I could never quite keep track. He was a pretty smart kid, tall for his age and skinny. Right now, he was a scared seven or eight-year-old. I pried him away from me and squatted in front of him. The beginnings of a shiner had started on the left side of his face and eye.

"Hey buddy, what's goin' on?"

"He's come back." He sniffled and wiped his nose on his wet sleeve. "He came back, and I told him that we didn't want him to come back. He threw me out and slammed the door."

"He's back? Who's come back?"

His lips trembled and his voice dropped. "Jake."

"How? How's he back? I thought he was gone for good."

"He's come back for mom. He said she has to go with him."

"I thought he was going to leave the country, or at least the state."

"He said he's gotta go, and he wants mom to go with him. Him and his buddies."

"He's got someone with him?"

"Two or three guys. They stole somethin'."

"Okay pal, let's get you warmed up and I guess I need

to go have a talk with Mr. Jake."

"No Uncle Emmett. He said if you show up, he'll hurt my mom. He told me that he's gonna kill you and Uncle Andy someday."

"Well, we'll just see about that."

By this time Angie had arrived in the front hallway too. I looked at both of them. The look on their faces spoke volumes. Tears were in Angie's eyes.

Dutch looked at me and shook her head. "You should call the police Emmett." Dutch was trying to be firm, but she knew I wouldn't do any such thing. "Let's get him in a hot shower and then put him in one of the beds to warm him up."

"Have you had dinner yet Grant?" Angie was catching up too.

"No, I came straight here. I wanted to go to grandpa's but it's too far. Am I ever gonna see my mom again Angie?"

"You bet buddy. Let's get you squared away first though okay?"

I went into the kitchen, and took the phone off the wall and dialed my brother.

"Hello?"

"It's Emmett. Jake's back in town, he's at Kelly's."

"Shit, he doesn't listen very well. How'd you find out?"

"Grant's here, walked all the way in the rain. Geez, must be almost 4 miles and in this weather. Jake's brought a posse with him. Says he's come to take Kelly and skedaddle. He threw Grant out."

"What a douchebag! I'll get my stuff. Pick me up."

"One more thing…"

"What's that?"

"Says he wants you dead buddy."

"Oh yeah? Well like Da says, 'that door swings both ways'. How do ya' want'ta handle it?"

"Guess I'll call Da."

"If you do that, you know what's gonna happen right?"

"Kinda gonna go that way anyway Andy."

Jake Brennan was a nickel-dime criminal from the old neighborhood. He was the victim of his own fantasies, never quite able to pull off the big score that he could imagine in his head. Either he was a poor planner, and enlisted the wrong help, or he was just plain stupid. I always leaned him toward the last choice. His main weakness was my sister Kelly Casey, now Kelly Donovan, whom he had adored since they had been in second grade together.

When Kelly had married Tom Donovan and had given birth to Grant, Jake had almost lost his mind. When Tom had then been diagnosed with an aggressive cancer and succumbed in just three short months, Jake had thought it was a sign from God that they were to be together forever. The only problem that stood in his way was that Kelly just could not stand him.

Jake's efforts to woo Kelly had become increasingly desperate, and eventually, he just resorted to violence. The beatings had gone on for a while, unbeknownst to the rest of us in the family, that is until Kelly had ended up in the Emergency Room. One look at Kelly, with her arm in a sling and bruised face was all it had taken for my father, Little Mick Casey, to go dark.

Mick Casey had never been accused of being much of a conversationalist by even the greatest stretch of the imagination, but when he was angry his quiet demeanor became malevolent. Even as children we knew not to step into his headlights when he was mad. The difference this time however was instead of dealing with it quietly and by himself, he stepped back and turned to us.

"You two are gonna handle this."

"Fine with me."

"Me too" Andy's response only a half-second behind my own.

"If I go, I'm gonna kill someone. I don't know how to be clever about that sort of thing."

"Oh, like I do Da?"

He had just fixed me with that look he was capable of doing, one eyebrow raised and the opposite eye aimed directly at me. He used it whenever I or anyone else had said something stupid.

"Okay Da, but I don't want to kill him either."

"Speak for yourself." Andy was hot.

I looked at Kelly sitting in the hospital bed. Her bright blue eyes were red from crying, and the bruise on her face was swelling the left one shut. The look in her eyes was one of fear. Just as we turned to leave the room, my older sister Kate breezed by the nurse.

She took one look at Kelly, turned to Da with a frown, "Da?"

"R.E. and Andy are going to see to it."

"They better—or I will."

It had taken the two us the better part of the night to find the son-of-a-bitch. It was unfortunate that somehow in his haste to avoid us, he had managed to fall down an entire flight of stairs—twice.

His luck didn't improve after that either. When he arrived at the hospital by ambulance, he was handcuffed to the gurney by the police officers waiting there for him. He was arrested as soon as he was discharged. Kelly had pressed charges and testified. He was also curiously enough, found to be in possession of several items of high value and which were listed as stolen by the burglary division. They also confiscated an illegal sawed-off shotgun, which I will miss dearly. It had translated into a lengthy vacation down at Joliet State Prison with 'three hots and a cot'.

He must have copped a pretty sweet plea deal in order to be out already, it hadn't been three years since the trial date. Even with time served before he was convicted, he was out early. His arrival at Kelly's last night was probably one of the dumbest things he could have ever done. There must certainly be a restraining order still in effect, but to risk another traumatic accident like the last one was bordering on incredibly stupid. It also meant he must be planning on moving very quickly.

I picked up Andy at his place. He reached across and punched me in the shoulder, his usual form of greeting for me. He also dropped a set of knuckles into my lap and dropped another set into the pocket of his old fatigue jacket. Together we wheeled across town to my father's house. In the driveway at my father's house, I looked at Andy. His eyebrows were furrowed and his hands were clenching and unclenching. Da walked out to the car; he wasn't in a hurry. It was a very familiar walk to both of us, deliberate and heavy with malice. It was a reminder of childhood fear and hard spankings.

We both stepped out and met him at the hood of the car.

"Well?"

"We're gonna go have a talk with him. If we have to chase, we might be gone for awhile Da."

"You better goddamn do more than have a talk R.E."

"Got that right." Andy's voice was tight, angry.

We walked back to the car and I opened the door, but he tapped me on the shoulder and raised a finger.

"Wait here a minute."

He came back in less than a minute, carrying something hanging by a cord in his hand.

"Here, I made these for you boys. Was supposed to be a surprise but, who knows, might be handy."

He handed one to me and one to Andy.

"What the hell?"

"They're just like mine, but nicer. I used parachute cord and got silver mouthpieces for 'em. They're pretty don't ya' think?"

By the light of the streetlight, I looked at the one he'd handed to me. A cattle horn, over a foot-and-a-half long with a slight curl. The open end had been bronzed and polished; the narrow end was wrapped in fine woven cord with a silver bugle mouthpiece. It was a battle horn and a nice one.

"Blow it."

"What? Here?"

When we were young my father would take his horn into the woods when he took us hunting. He would find a high spot, deep in the forest. Once there he would lay his gun down and take off his pack, spread his legs and wind the horn. The blast was so loud in the silence of the woods it would echo through the hills for half a minute and cause the hair on our arms, legs and the backs of our necks to stand straight up. When he did that his eyes would flame, and he would throw his head back with a great shout then would blow the horn again and again until his knees weakened from the effort.

"Blow it."

Andy looked at me and shrugged. He raised it to his lips and gave a blow. The result was a mellow hoot.

"What the fuck was that? I said blow it not fart into it."

Andy had studied trumpet in grade school and his second effort showed the hours of practice he'd squandered on the instrument; it rattled windows and probably hastened the deliveries of any maternity cases in the neighborhood.

"Holy shit! That is awesome! Wow!"

"Wow's right. We gotta get outta here after that, it's gonna piss somebody off."

"Yep, it's time to go boys; the Casey's are goin' hunting."

"What? I thought you weren't going?"

"I changed my mind."


Kelly and Tom Donovan had bought a small three-bedroom ranch house a little way out of town on a wooded one-acre lot. Tom had loved cutting wood and working the yard, and there had been enough sun along the south side of the house to have a kitchen garden for Kelly. With the birth of Grant, it seemed that their life was on a trajectory of happiness. All that had changed with Tom's illness, and the house had become too much for Kelly to manage with a small boy and left-over hospital bills. We had all pitched in when we could, but the truth had been clear. Without Tom's income and with the shortfall of his health insurance, Kelly was deeply in debt and trapped in a house she couldn't afford.

When Jake Brennan had arrived on the scene he had at first seemed nice enough. He had paid some of Kelly's bills and wasn't entirely clumsy with household repairs. But that had changed quickly. Kelly still steeped in grief, was not ready or interested in a romance. The fact that she didn't like Jake didn't help either. Soon enough, Jake just resorted to taking his romance by force, and that had precipitated his unfortunate encounter with the staircase.

The steady rain had tapered off to a misty drizzle, and fog had started to rise out of the still frozen ground of spring. There was no wind, and the drip of water was the only sound in the woods. It was still too early for frogs or crickets to be awake yet. The house was secluded enough so that it was easier to telephone the neighbors than to walk to their house. Once we arrived, we wouldn't be disturbed. As we approached the house on the road, we could see the front door was wide open and the light from inside spilled out into the front yard. Shadows moved in and out of the doorway, and a car sat in the driveway with parking lights on.

"Drive on past and then let me out." Andy was patting his pockets in the back seat.

"Got everything you need?"

"I'm outta cigarettes; got any?"

"No smoking while you're huntin'." Da was directing the event. "Take the horn, wait until I blow mine then give it a hoot. Got it?"

"Yep, think it'll work."

"It has before."

"What?"

"Never mind, just get out at the edge of the woods, head around to the shed out in back."

"Roger that. Watch your six."

"You too."

I parked the car about a half mile farther down the

road in a small lane that disappeared along an old barbed wire fence line and made ready to walk back to the house. The fog was already thick enough, so the house back down the road had disappeared.

"You comin'?"

"In a minute."

"Suit yourself. If this goes south go for the cops Da."

"That'll be the day. I'm needing to think of a way to let Kelly know we're here."

"Pretty sure she's gonna figure it out Da."

"She's probably pretty worried about Grant and scared too."

"I know, it's what I been thinkin' about too."

I opened the door and stepped out into the lane. I already had my knife strapped to my back pocket and I reached back in to pick up my .38 Ruger.

"No guns tonight boy. Leave it."

I looked up at him in the passenger seat. His face lit by the overhead light of the car. His lips were in a tight line, and his dark eyes flashed. I knew that look all too well.

I left the gun but picked up the horn.

Walking back toward the house I stayed off the road and on the shoulder. I didn't want to risk a heel strike on the pavement or a stumble over a stone to alert anyone to my presence. The fog would magnify any sound I made. As I neared the house, I could hear men's loud voices as they moved in and out of the house, just out of sight in the trees. When I got to the mailbox at the end of the drive I crouched down and tried to get a count of how many of them there actually were. The sound of my truck starting surprised me and I swiveled on my heels to see it back out onto the road with its bright headlights shining through the foggy night and race back down the road toward me.

As the truck approached, it braked and swung into the driveway, throwing gravel and fishtailing toward the house. Finally sliding to a stop in a spray of gravel directly behind the two parked cars and blocking their exit. The driver's side door swung open and my father hit the ground at a dead run directly at the nearest silhouette. Even with his small stature, the collision brought the surprised individual to the ground. Da was immediately astride him and laying into him with both fists.

Two of the other men raced to the aid of their partner and dragged Da off and to his feet. The beaten fellow was slow to get up, but once he was on his feet, he immediately gave my father a powerful haymaker to the solar plexus and another left across the jaw. Da slumped, apparently unconscious. The two assistants dragged him to the house and inside. The commotion had all happened within a half-minute and caught me by surprise. I had moved halfway up the lane before realizing that I was out in the open and exposed.

Retreating across the drive and into the brush along the edge of the woods, I hunkered down and looked around. I still needed a census count.

In the house, Mick Casey sat in a kitchen chair and watching the proceedings. His daughter Kelly stood next to him, staunching the blood that seeped from the corner of his mouth. In the living room Jake Brennan and three other men weighed and separated into plastic bags a large amount of white powder. They were moving quickly, agitated by the arrival of Mick and fueled by the paranoia that a nose full of cocaine brings. They had been in a hurry before but now it seemed that even more haste was called for.

Jake's nose was stuffed full of toilet paper that had begun to turn red. His lip was already puffing up and leaking blood that he continually licked off and his left eye had already started to swell shut.

Mick caught Kelly's hand and stopped it. His hard eyes met her deep blue ones and he smiled up at her.

"It's okay, your Da's here for you now."

"Oh Daddy, you can't be here; you shouldn't be here."

"What? Not come and get you darlin'; these pissants got nothin' to offer that I'm worried about."

"That right you old fucker? How bout I shoot a nice round hole in that stubborn head of yours? Think that might make you a little more respectful." Jake's consonants were seriously compromised by his plugged nose.

Mick shook his head and licked his bleeding lip, "A little dipshit like you? It'd take a few more of you than's here tonight."

In two steps Jake crossed the room and slammed his fist down on Mick's left ear.

"Shut the fuck up! You shouldn't've come and now that you did, well that's just a fuckin' shame, cuz we ain't takin' ya' with us. Capiche?"

"I don't speak none of that eye 'talion shit. We'll see who sleeps tonight and where."

"Oh yes. That we will. I only wish I had a couple more of you fuckin' Casey's here. Man, we'd have graves to dig. Yep, it'd be a shindig. Haha, oh yes we would."

"Maybe they're already here?"

"What? What're you talkin' about?"

"We'll see."

"Shut the fuck up!"

Jake strode to the front, slapping the overhead light switch off as he passed by. Peering out into the darkness, he cupped his hands without the light behind him.

"That you out there Andy? How 'bout it Emmett you around? I don't give a shit, do you hear me? Not one god-damned-fucking shit. If'n you guys wanna try and come and get me, there's two Caseys in here that will each get a bullet in the noggin' the second I set eyes on either one of ya'"

There was only silence in answer.

Mick nudged Kelly with his elbow. When she looked at him in horror, he winked and nodded.

"Now m'darlin', now you're gonna see somethin."

From outside the unholy two-note blast of the war horn tore through the night.

Inside the house, the four men and one women froze. Kelly's fingers dug into Mick's shoulder.

"What the heck is that Da?"

"Ssshh now, best you sit on the floor for a bit Missy, here right next to me."

"What the fuck?! What the fuck was that? Mick what the fuck."

"Well my friends, sounds like the posse's arrived." Mick slid out of the chair onto the floor next to Kelly and crossed his arms.

"What the fuck, didn't you guys check the back seat of that truck? Who's out there Mick, is it Emmett, or Andy? Don't know which one I'd like to kill more."

"I don't know Jake, never heard any of my kids blow a fuckin' horn like that. Must be somebody else – maybe."

"Trace, get out there and check the car. Take a gun. If

it's a Casey, shoot first."

"Why do I haveta' go? I don't wanna fuck with those Casey boys."

"Just shoot 'em. Tony, slip out the back, come down along the side of the house. Keep an eye out and cover Trace. Oh god, if it's a Casey we just about got us a jackpot."

Tony, grabbed up a large automatic and headed for the back door. He had just put his hand on the back door handle when another long blast of the battle horn split the night. This time the terrifying sound came from behind the house.

Tony let go of the door handle like it was hot, and backed away from it.

"Geezus! What the hell is that noise?"

Another, blast of the horn from the front of the house, and then both in unison, one in front and one in back.

"We gotta get outta here!"

"Shut up, it's them goddamn Casey's that's for sure. Nobody else does shit like this. Look at the old fucker, grinnin' from ear-to-ear, you die first motherfucker. You guys start baggin' this shit up; we'll go when I say we go."

Another long blast from the horns, both front and back, layer upon layer of sound that continued for over a minute.

"I don't care! I can't do this! I can't man. I gotta get outta here Jake."

"You go, you don't get no cut. You're out."

"I don't care, I don't wanna find out who's blowin' that horn. I'm gone man."

The terrified druggie went to the front door and flung it open. With his hands up, he stepped out into the darkness.

"Hey! Hey out there! I got my hands up; I'm comin' out. Hey, hey…

From inside the house, it appeared he had stopped to wait for a response as he paused just outside the door. But slowly, he tipped back on his heels, his head and shoulders reentering the room as he fell slowly at first, and then rapidly backward, landing in a sodden unconscious thud on the threshold. A massive bloody wound had appeared over his right eye, and his sightless eyes stared across at Mick and Kelly.

"Rock?" Kelly asked

"Appears so." Mick's calm reply

Again, the horns blew, and again they blew for over a minute.

"Geezus Jake, who the fuck are these people?"

"That fucker over there's Mick Casey, and those motherfuckers out there are probably Emmett and Andy Casey. This slut is his daughter and their sister."

"Fuck me! You mean it's goddam fuckin' 'Hole' Casey?"

"The one and only."

"Man, I don't want to get crosswise with Hole Casey, he'll fuck us all up. I seen it. I seen what he does Jake."

"If it's any consolation to you, Andy's probably worse."

"And they're both out there?" This time he directed the question to Mick.

"Would seem so, yes. I'm afraid you guys are in for a time of it."

"We'll see about that. Get up old man, you and me, we're gonna go out and have a little talk with your boys. This ends right here, right now."

"Too right." Mick started to push himself up from the floor, but before he could get all the way upright, the lights all went out and the house was pitched into midnight blackness as the power was cut to the entire house. Almost immediately, the horns blew again, and again, and again.

"Don't try anything Mick! I got this bitch by her pretty red hair and I'll cut her ear-ta-ear. Ya' got it?"

Silence

"Did ya hear Mick? Answer me, don't get fuckin' cute with me."

Silence

"I'm givin' you to the count of three Mick, answer me."

Mick's voice spoke from deep in the far corner of the room.

"You boys in here yet?"

"Yes Da."

"I'm here too Da."

"Well boys, let's get down to business."

# The Suitcase

## Ana Manwaring

You're such a card, Mortie. A funny guy. Sixty-seven years of marriage you still make me laugh. I've never regretted a day of it–even though your father-the-Rabbi was against the wedding—too young, he said. But Grandmother Sigler and your aunt–what was her name? The yenta. They convinced him, and there we were smashing fancy cups at that new Max Strauss Center over on West Wilson. You remember the one—opened before the war.

So handsome you were in your tuxedo with that curly black hair slicked back and shining. And I was a queen in my gown—imagine, lace all the way from Italy. *Shana maidel*. That's what you said when you saw me. Beautiful girl. And you promised me right then and there that you'd take me to all the beautiful places in the world, like

Niagara Falls, because *beauty belonged with beauty*.

You'd just bought the butcher shop in Skokie and you had to travel for an hour on the streetcar to get to work. We were poor, then, weren't we, Mortie? Too poor to go all the way to Niagara Falls for a honeymoon—but enough for Elkhart Lake in Wisconsin.

You bought that leather-covered suitcase, almost a steamer trunk it was so big. "What! You planning on shipping yourself somewhere," I asked you? *Big enough for both of us*, you answered.

I remember it like it was yesterday, Mort. How the Siebkins welcomed us in and gave us the best room in the house overlooking the lake. All that clear blue water—what we saw of it. I saw a lot of you, Mortie, and so much to see! We said we'd go to Niagara Falls as soon as we saved enough money.

But God has his plans and two years later I was nursing our first bundle of joy, Rachel—you named her after your grandmother—and you shipped out to France with the United States Army, Mort, hauling that big brown suitcase. I ran the shop with Mr. Lipinsky. You did good with him as a partner. He was a charmer, that one. Soon we had matrons lining up to buy our meat. We always had meat what with Mr. Lipinsky's connections. A real *macher* he was! When Cohen's and Buchet's barely had a side of beef, we had it all. And I saved every dime from the shop and from the upstairs apartment so when you got back from the war, we could go to Niagara Falls.

Mama—may she rest in peace—kept Rachel after you were wounded. Neighbors at the synagogue took up a collection, flew me to London to stay with you while you recovered. Such kind people they were—people aren't like that anymore, Mortie.

And you in that Army hospital. I was so worried. *Won't be dancing the Hora too soon*, you said. You tried to teach the steps to the little English nurses, but I saw how that wooden foot hurt you. But you're a funny guy, Mortie. You just kept telling the jokes about the landmines and the French and the Generals—making all those poor wounded soldiers laugh. And left foot or no left foot, you still had it in you. Or as you liked to say, you still had it in me.

You were behind the lines nine months later when the twins joined the family. Your father-the-Rabbi was so pleased that we chose his given name, Caleb, for the boy. And Mama, she told all the customers, "Such a fine son-in-law, naming his girl after his mother-in-law." *Oi! Gevalt!* Who was to know that Judith would turn out to be a lesbian? It would have killed her grandmother if she'd lived to see the day.

Caleb was funny just like his father. Two comedians under one roof, I had. And he's a doctor. A mother should be so lucky. So much love, so much laughter. We almost forgot about Niagara Falls, didn't we, Mortie? *Sparrow*, you'd say—you always called me Sparrow. Said I reminded you of a delicate bird. You card, Mortie. After five children? But you said, *Sparrow, we have everything we need. We have a good life, we have each other, Niagara Falls will wait.*

After the war you bought-out Mr. Lipinsky's share from the butcher shop. He moved away from Chicago, something about living closer to his daughter who had married a rancher from Colorado. I never did hear if he opened that new shop out in Denver, but I guess he'd have had a steady supply of beef. Buffalo too, I hear. Probably not *kosher*.

We had that little apartment at the back of Mama's house. Remember how cozy it was with the children? Yes, it was crowded, if that's the way you remember it, but we stayed there until Hannah came along in '48. You were always gone working in those first years after Mr. Lipinsky left, and Mama played cards with her friends all day. *Oi Vey!* Me with only babies for company. I needed something to do and you, my generous Mortimer, agreed to give the upstairs tenants notice and move us in over the shop in time for Rachel to start school in Skokie. But all our savings went to fixing up the apartment and buying a car and we couldn't go on vacation. *Next year,* you promised. *Next year we'll drive the whole family out to Niagara Falls.*

That was the year your mother died from the cancer. We couldn't go away and leave your poor father. I worried he wouldn't make it through the funeral and it was the first time in your life you didn't have a joke. Not until Little Mortie was born. That baby lit up your father-the-Rabbi like I never saw him. Gave him something to live for.Speaking of the funeral, you remember Anshe Zedek? I heard his wife just dropped dead in the checkout line at the *kosher* market over on Oakton. I'm not surprised, that man was tight. Probably squeezed her to death. What was her name? But Anshe was a good businessman you always told me. I wasn't so sure about buying into his market on the other side of town. You cut the meat at both shops—all that running around you had to do. And with only one foot. I took over the selling in our shop as soon as the twins went to school. We made more money, but we were too busy to take our trip to New York that year.

Then we sold out to that chain. That was the year we went to the Catskills. Packed your old leather covered suitcase and put all the kids into the Chevy and drove across the country to that resort, what was it called? You remember, Mortie, everybody wanted to see that new comedian, Mel Brooks. Now *he* was a funny guy. You told his jokes over and over. And Rachel met her first boyfriend. How can we forget that? A *goy*, you said, and your father-the-Rabbi, tuning over in his grave. Later Rachel ran off with some poet to San Francisco. Did I mention we got a postcard from her? We talked about going to visit in San Francisco, but with two new shops, we couldn't get away.

Life was good, you always said, and we worked hard, didn't we, Mortie? We saved and planned for our retirement. Little Mortie would take over the business. We would finally go to Niagara Falls for our retirement celebration. We'd take the kids and the grandkids. But when the time came, you and Little Mortie sold one of the shops and expanded into health foods. *The wave of the future*, you said. You said you couldn't see yourself with nothing to do. Sitting down in front of a television set would kill you. You still using all those knives and meat cutters–and already missing a foot, but you two comedians just made a joke and went on with business as usual. I packed that old suitcase and flew to Miami to stay with my sister.

Hannah came to bring me home. Caleb sent her. He was worried about you. Little Mortie said you'd been acting funny at the shop. Said you were forgetting things, not making sense with the customers. You said, *Sparrow, that's a load of bunk. I'm fit as a fiddle and I don't need you noodging me. You're just mad because we didn't go to Niagara Falls. I'll tell you what Sparrow*, you said, *let's go. Call and make a reservation tomorrow and we'll fly out there together, just the two of us.* But I told you to go to the neurologist before I'd go off on a vacation. "Call Caleb," I said.

So what's funny about a brain tumor? You were the

only one making the jokes. The doctor said you didn't have much longer, but Mortie, you said you weren't dead yet and we were going to Niagara Falls. Marched right out of that medical office and called the airlines. *Sparrow*, you said, *we're going to Niagara Falls.* You said, *Promise me, Sparrow. No matter what.*

Mortie, I promised, and the taxi is on its way. You're packed in that old suitcase, but you took up so much room I could hardly find a spot for my nightgown. Our honeymoon suitcase, Mortie, do you remember? This will be our second honeymoon.*Feh*! A *schmuk*, the driver is. Mortie, he says it stinks in our apartment—like rotten meat. What's the matter with the young people today? I told him to *shlep* your suitcase downstairs and mind his own business. He looked at the suitcase and asked me, "Are you cleaning out Dad's things? You were supposed to call me to help."

*Genug es genug*, Mortie. I told him to stop with the *kvetching* already! I said, "Just carry the suitcase to the taxi. My husband and I are on our way to Niagara Falls."

# Trigger

## Lisa Towles

*Three screams. That's all it took; all it ever took. She knew him by now, the funny way the right side of his mouth twitched when he tried not to cry, the involuntary blink of his left eye the moment evil re-entered his body. It came from the ground, welling up from his dark nethered past like a hole opening in the cold ground, traveling up his limbs, pulsing in his hands, the oily presence sliding over him like a worn, smelly jacket that feels like home.*

*"Don't scream, Berry, just don't scream," he'd always say. "No one's gonna hear you anyway, because old Sly thinks of everything."*

*Not everything.*

*She'd made a study of him, the years of stained, tangled sheets draped onto the scuffed floors like her wedding gown had been once, twenty lifetimes ago when he'd loved her. He did, too, and not just that night. His love for her was his liability now, and her weapon of choice. She used it, honed it, manipulated it to pierce the core of his composure at the right times. Tonight was different, special. Black heels special, lace underwear special, all his favorites. She bought them for the occasion two months in advance, along with all the other accoutrements of sin. Thou shall not kill. She even bought a new Bible, not to mock him but to reward herself for what she knew would be her biggest moment of courage.*

"You ready for this?" Kathy asked her at their typical breakfast table in the corner of the cafeteria.

But Berry's thoughts were of her own house this morning, and how peaceful she'd felt rocking in the hammock she'd positioned in her living room over the white, tiled floor. Her indoors-hammock in a room and a house with a lock on the door and only one key. She still hadn't furnished it with much else because there wasn't time during the day, when he was working. But it was a beginning, a whole new world built from a single intention.

"I'm just talking to people; it's no big deal."

Kathy reached across their plates and grabbed her. "Who do you think you're talking to? Do you think I don't know the truth just because the police haven't figured it out?"

Berry Raskin tried not to spit up the eggs in her mouth. Kathy had no proof of anything because there wasn't any. No evidence of assault, foul play, nothing but the fingerprints and forensic material that would normally be present in the house of a cohabitating husband and wife.

"What are you gonna tell them today, these impressionable women? Desperate, that's what they are, just like you used to be." Kathy's voice nagged, whined almost, her round face scrunched into an unnatural shape. "You're gonna teach them how to kill?"

"Are you crazy?" Berry snapped. "Now why would I do that? Sly's not even dead."

"Maybe not medically, but he'll never recover. The doctors said so."

Kathy was right about that part; he wouldn't ever recover. She'd planned it that way with the foresight and meticulous preparation of a serial killer covering her tracks. But luckily for her, this crime was victimless with no provable evidence. And there would never be any.

*Berry Raskin bought a pillow, a set of two at the mall, these king-sized, overstuffed jobs thick enough to muffle sound and thin enough to fold in half for double insulation. She practiced with them, screaming in the back of her bedroom closet so the neighbors didn't hear her during the daytime hours, adjusting her screams, the length, duration, volume, while Sly was at work and she was locked in the bedroom without food or water. No bathroom. He cooked them dinner when he got home. He'd cooked in the military, early on, before he rose up Marine ranks, and knew how to pull a meal together quickly. She'd eat politely and ask about his day, gently stroking the time bomb and all the while observing every tick of his behavior. Did he actually think she stayed in that room all day without food or water, without relieving herself, and expect her to be fine night after night when he unlocked the door with that long, grotesque skeleton key? He did, she knew he did, because Sly had a tell for everything.*

*This morning at her usual time of seven-thirty, Berry made sure Sly's car was gone from the driveway, then opened the closet door and pulled up the carpet and the subfloor panel, a rectangle large enough to fit her hundred-pound frame, and lowered herself into the basement, where she kept gallons of water stored behind the washer and dryer, along with crackers, granola bars, pens, and a journal. She drank water straight from the heavy plastic jug until she couldn't drink any more, slipped one granola bar in her jacket pocket, and stared thoughtfully at the journal. She opened it, fingered the pages, observed the tiny print she'd been using so it would last until she got out, but closed it again knowing anything she wrote after tonight would be her demise. Because tonight Sly Raskin was going to die.*

*Sometimes she'd sneak out the broken window in the garage and walk three cold miles in thin shoes to the shelter near Howard Street in San Francisco. Rawanda, who did the onboardings, always smiled at her with stained, crooked teeth in a way that made her feel like a starlet getting out of a limousine. "There's my Berry Girl," she'd say with her face all lit up, welcoming her back from the caverns of hell, her only real respite. Sly had to know that someone had helped clean the wounds on her face, bandaged her bruised hands and fingernails. But he never mentioned it, maybe because he didn't want to acknowledge her betrayal. Or maybe keeping that demon locked in the cage in his heart took every ounce of his waking energy.*

*Kathy Marr, one of the shelter counselors, had a mane of red hair and strong hands that had more than once grabbed her bony shoulders and urged her to go to the police. And it's not that they didn't understand the cycle of domestic abuse there. They specialized in it, built programs around self-empowerment and transformation, offered group and 1:1 therapy for survivors in every stage. Sly was just different, that's all.*

*After his military discharge, his doctors said he suffered from* misophonia, extreme aversion to certain noises, and for Sly it was loud, shrill sounds. He never talked much about the Gulf War or Afghanistan, but he served one tour in each and came back emotionally impenetrable. Almost like he no longer had emotions, the cords somehow cut by some thing, some memory. But she knew the secret button that unlocked Sly's forbidden black box – a human scream. In the span of one breath, he could go from a tall, solid, blocky soldier to a trembling madman beyond control. One year ago tonight, ten years after his honorable discharge, Sly came home and startled Berry in the kitchen, causing her to scream and a dinner plate to crash on the floor. His face, at the sound of it, turned pink, eyes wide, rage pulsing in his trembling hands.

"What's the matter with you?" she asked, terrified at the sight of this other person taking over. She kept screaming, couldn't help it.

"Stop screaming. Just stop. Please. Stop." His voice was calm, but tears slid down his cheeks. Her screams turned to sobs as she looked for a way out of the room. Sly used his body to block her path. "Get away from the door." He moved forward and grabbed her around her thin waist, hucked her head and shoulders over his back and carried her to the bedroom, threw her on the bed, and climbed on top of her while she shrieked, his palms struggling to subdue the sounds coming from her mouth, like he might die if he didn't. He sat on her, then kneeled on her legs to keep her from running.

Berry tried to avert her eyes from this Marvel comic book figure, half expecting his head to explode all over the room. Had she taken something, some kind of herb or hallucinogen? Could you even do that by accident? Who was this creature on top of her? By instinct she kept her legs clamped tight but knew, somehow, rape was the farthest thing from his mind. First there were slaps, on her face and head, then when her shrieks grew louder he used his fists. Blood spurted from her lips when he *cracked her jaw and cheeks, a splash of her own blood and mucus on the white wall now dripping beneath the window. It kept going the more she cried and screamed.*

*That first time resulted in two missing teeth and a cut on her left eye that never fully healed. She didn't eat anything for a week. How she didn't die of malnutrition fascinated her, in those long empty days in the quiet house, alone with her pen and journal, her only companions. No, of course she couldn't call the police. What would he do to her? And she hadn't yet discovered the shelter back then. She felt too ashamed to go to her brother's place because he was a successful business exec in an ivory tower, buffered by a high salary, his own driver, and handlers. Where would she even begin?*

They'd finished dinner with minimal small talk. Sometimes Sly filled the silence by reciting the events from his day working at a machine shop, stories of his dysfunctional boss, quirky coworkers, equipment failures, and docked pay. Other times he ate, flinched at the clink of cutlery against their white China plates, waiting, watching her, expecting something that never came. And all the while Berry was doing the same, cataloging his eye movements, finger taps, chewing practices in the invisible notebook she kept in her head, creating her unofficial criminal profile of Marine Sergeant Sly Raskin. Usually the sounds of dinner cleanup unraveled him, in combination with three or four beers, and he'd pull her into the bedroom for their twice weekly ritual. If her wounds became too grotesque, he'd sometimes will himself to sleep at the kitchen table, unable to cope with the reality of the new war he'd created.

Her friends at the shelter, the people who came to her room, huddled around her bed, dabbed alcohol on her face and clasped her hand in their warm palms, begged her to stay there with them, vowing to protect her with their devotion and, if needed, the law. Kathy Marr had a blue and yellow silk scarf wrapped around her auburn hair today and tiny, silver earrings that lit up her face with sparkles.

"Don't do it, girl."

"Do what?" Berry ignored her and kept walking toward the cafeteria, where she knew they served chicken noodle soup on Tuesdays, a comforting vestige of early childhood. She stood in a small line and carried her bowl on a tray to a far two-seater by the window. Kathy followed and sat in the other chair, staring back with her sideways grin. She'd always reminded Berry of Pam Grier in the film *Jackie Brown*, all dolled up with makeup and smart pantsuits. Was that what she herself lacked, even more than beauty? Jackie Brown had presence. An almost cocky confidence of knowing who she is and what she's capable of. Kathy Marr carried herself like she was in control of her life and the world met her requests, no questions asked. Didn't hurt that she was five foot nine either.

"What are you doing, girl? And don't say nothing to me. There's only one way out of the hell you're in right now, and that's the legal way. It's hard, and it's scary, and that's what this organization is all about." Kathy leaned in. A waft of cigarette smoke and Vanilla perfume filled the air. "Whatever you're planning, just don't."

"Don't do what?" Berry shot back, annoyed now but

still playing dumb. "Leave me alone to enjoy my soup."

"Someone saw you yesterday," Kathy whispered. "With a bag of pillows. What do you think I'm thinking?"

"Sly has trouble sleeping. I got him, well, both of us, some new pillows. What's the issue?" Berry panicked at how easily the lie came out, especially to someone she trusted, maybe even loved. But she wasn't trusting Kathy. No one would know because there would be no evidence, and no one would understand anyway. Only she understood what unlocked the demon living inside Sly Raskin, and only she knew how to kill it.

Berry found Special Agent Romeo Gomez getting coffee at the Starbucks one building over from San Francisco's FBI field office. In her time held captive in the house during the day, she'd borrowed a friend's old laptop and was able to research members of Sly's U.S. Marines Platoon and Company from Afghanistan, his last and worst tour. Like so many former-military, Gomez became Staff Sergeant in the Marines and, post-discharge, transitioned directly into the FBI training academy and became a Special Agent in six months. She'd messaged him from his email posted on the website with a phony query about women in the FBI. Sure, he replied back. He'd be happy to meet with her.

"Eileen?" Gomez asked, rising from a small, round table by the front door, coffee in one hand.

She'd given him a fake name for protection. "Hi," she said and shook his hand. His eyes blinked back, carefully assessing her trustworthiness, then scanned her from top to bottom. They sat. He sipped. She crossed her legs and hooked her handbag on the back of the chair.

"Eileen who?"

"Raskin," she said and waited. He got it right away.

"Sly?" he asked with a smile that faded in two seconds. "You his sister or something? How's he doing?"

"He's not well, and I need to know what happened to him out there. I've done some research. You were with him in Iraq and Afghanistan. Something happened there. I need to know," she paused to breathe. "So I can help him. He needs help." It all sounded so altruistic out here in broad daylight, the man's earnest face staring back, remembering, obviously, how broken Sly had been. He bought the story. So far.

Gomez nodded, drained his cup and set it on the table. "I got something." He examined the smooth black wood under his fingertips. "I need to see him, though. That's my price for sharing. Will you leave me his phone number or address?"

"Of course," she replied with no intention of actually doing it.

Gomez had to get back to work and suggested she walk him back through the grassy path behind the building. His face looked innocent as he suggested it, but something in her bones warned her.

"I actually need to get back in a few minutes. Can you tell me here?"

"Sure," he said and motioned for them to talk outside in the street. "Address first." He held out his hand.

Berry nodded and reached into her cavernous purse. She wrote down the first address that came to her outside of San Francisco – the public library address in Sacramento, where she'd worked years ago, so she knew it from memory.

"Sly lives in Sacramento? But he hates the heat." He

looked at the ground. "Those of us who…"

Berry snapped her purse shut and crossed her arms across her chest, moving an inch closer. "What happened to him?"

"Okay," he nodded and took a breath. "He was captured. There was a ground conflict, called the Battle of Khafji. Sly was captured by Afghani fighters, *mujahideen*, with two others from our Company and brought to a cell, exposed to chemical warfare—"

"Like nerve gas?" Berry asked.

"Yeah that, also blister agents. Terrible. They had him in a cell with two others, and they were next to a cell with two women, one of them was about to give birth and wouldn't stop screaming. I think the other woman was trying to deliver the baby, God knows what she would have done with it if--"

"If?"

"Women captives didn't fare well, still don't, I'm sure. Anyway, the two women in the cell wouldn't stop screaming." Gomez shifted his feet, buttoned his jacket, and crossed his arms, now leaning into Berry but from the side, protecting himself from his own memories. "They shot her," he said and wiped his suddenly runny nose.

"The pregnant woman?" Berry asked. "And the baby?"

"They shot her in the stomach and the head, killing both of them." Gomez recited the words mechanically, and his face was stone. Berry fell to her knees, half out of shock, the other half in compassion for Sly having witnessed this depravity. Then again, there had likely been worse. Maybe much worse.

"Then the other woman started screaming," Gomez continued. "So as I understand it from the other two soldiers, there was screaming in there, like literally screaming bloody murder for hours. They finally shot the other woman, who wouldn't stop screaming obscenities at the captors."

And in the same way that Berry had seen evil enter Sly's body before his attacks on her, evil entered her in that moment on the curb, standing under the high sun with Agent Romeo Gomez. An evil thought took root in her brain, and she now knew how to end Sly's reign of terror on her. She'd gone there to better understand her husband's private hell. Now finally she understood the trigger. And she was about to become one herself.

When Sly came home from work, he wore eight hours' worth of aggravation on his face. Perfect, as he'd be easier to unglue. Instead of finding Berry huddled on the floor near the space heater, the one luxury he allowed her in the bedroom, he opened the door to find her fully dressed, makeup even, wearing heels, an apron, dinner being pulled out of the oven. She'd even trained her facial muscles to feign comfort at the sight of him instead of the rope of terror that lived in her body.

"Thought I'd cook for us tonight," she said easily but knew he'd never trust her. She was counting on it. Avoiding his eyes, she kept her concentration on the dinner, knowing he was hungry for food and rest. Without asking if he needed time to get settled, she set two full plates on the table, knowing he'd probably smelled the roasted chicken on the way up the stairs. It made her sad, in that moment, that she'd cooked for him, for both of them every night years ago, before the beatings started, before the demon took root in his broken brain and tried to choke the life out of her. Why did you only recognize an idyllic time after it was long gone? She knew *that* Sly was long gone. Now the rest of him was about to be too.

"How'd you get out?" was all he had to say after sitting at the table.

"I didn't go out. These are the groceries you bought last weekend," she answered in her practiced neutral-voice, devoid of the spitting vitriol that took over her speech during the beatings or the numbed-over resignation she used at the shelter. From Sly's perspective, she probably sounded like someone else. Faking had always come easy to her, for some reason, a benefit and detriment. Tonight it was her lifeline.

They ate in silence. He devoured every bite, got a second helping from the stove without offering her any, all the while avoiding her eyes like they'd somehow turn him to stone. But he was already stone, wasn't he? Good, dinner was over. Time to clean up.

He knew something was up. Sly left the table and disappeared into the bathroom to take a shower, something he usually did in the mornings right before work, stepping down the creaky stairs in wet hair. Berry went through the invisible list in her head and timed her movements to start the clink of silverware and China as soon as the shower turned off. A smile threatened the corners of her mouth, but she controlled it, reminding herself that her survival depended on discipline and vigilance above all. The dishes were soapy and wet. Some water splashed on the floor, causing her to step over it and rotate her body to the right. She caught Sly's glance from the doorway to the bedroom, watching her, looking down at her black heels that she'd chosen for this occasion, probably wondering if she had something other than food on her mind. Nothing could be truer. It was an ancient look of longing she hadn't seen on his face in over a decade. The old Sly. She turned too quickly and the plate in her hand slipped down. She was able to prevent it from falling on the floor, but it crashed into the sink. The clap of China on porcelain was even louder than if it had hit the floor.

"I'm sorry! I'm sorry! I can't help it, don't hurt me." The instant tears she'd practiced flowed freely down her cheeks. Berry Raskin stood frozen at the kitchen sink in her best clothes and sexiest shoes, ready for battle.

"Stop screaming." He was in the doorway but inching closer.

"I-I-I broke the plate because I wasn't paying attention. I haven't--" she paused for effect, "I haven't cooked dinner in a long time." Now folded over in sobs, she began to wail from her belly, a guttural moan from deep in her fakest of hearts. "Stay away from me," she shrieked now, a louder, bolder tone emerging, when he took two steps closer, willing him with her mind to grab her, using her perfectly researched psychological profile. Come to me, Sly Raskin. You're going down.

"Shut-the fuck-up," he said, now just steps away from her.

She continued sobbing and reached up and grabbed another of the soapy plates, rinsing it under the water, jerking her head back every two seconds to gauge his distance, lapsing into her rehearsed histrionics. "Stay away! Stay away from me, I can't take it anymore!" The volume of her voice surprised her, almost unsure whether this was still play acting or some real emotion slipping out. All the better.

"Move away from the sink, Roberta."

Berry froze. He hadn't called her that since before their

wedding. She turned, face streaked with tears, eyes puffy. "Leave me alone. I'm not your punching bag anymore."

"Do you wanna break a plate over my head? Is that what you're planning?"

She tried not to laugh and instead shriveled her face in confusion. "Stay away," she repeated, continuing with the dishes. Then something snapped. Sly lunged and grabbed her, taking the bait, picked her up and headed toward the bedroom. Evil sliding back into his familiar bones, the evil that was Other-Sly. *Now or never.* He tossed her down onto the bed and she unleashed the first of her rehearsed screams. She'd been pregnant once, years ago, from another man, but she'd never given birth. But at the shelter, she'd seen it three or four times and knew what the screams sounded like. She lay on her back and held her belly and screamed as loud as her lungs would allow, doubling over like she was in pain. Sly leaped off the bed and stared, numb. Trembling.

"Stay-away-from-me," she shrieked, then swallowed to save her vocal cords. They still had more to do tonight.

"What are you – who are—" he stammered, obviously now stuck somewhere between San Francisco and that cell in Afghanistan.

"What's wrong with your eyes?" she asked in a weeping voice, like she still cared about his well-being. He reached up and touched them. She'd read about the chemical warfare symptoms, scrolled through pictures online. "Are they burning? Are they on fire? Why are they all red?" she lied. "And your skin. Does it feel like bugs are crawling around inside it? You just took a shower. What's wrong with your skin?"

"Don't you—" he started, squeezed his eyes shut then stopped himself as if a voice inside was guiding him now.

Berry inhaled deeply and unleashed scream number two, a deafening wall of sound combined with a litany of stay-away-from-me's.

Back on the bed, a new force took over him, lips contracted into a tiny dot, his large hands holding her arms down.

"Leave me alone, leave me alonnnne," she wailed, ending in sobs, coughs, and she struggled to release herself from his grip. If only she'd brought a cast iron frying pan into the bedroom. But that would be too easy, and only temporary. This was the long game, because there was no going back. Sly reached his right hand out to his side and brought his fist back in a funnel vortex to her face. One of her teeth flew out of her mouth, a top one, and her mouth filled with blood.

"Your eyes are on fire, what's wrong with them, Sly? Your skin's crawling with bugs inside it. Get off me, I'm having a baby. Stay away from my baby!" The words had been specifically chosen just for him, this moment.

Sly Raskin stood tall at the end of the bed, his face a mess of tangled emotion, scratching his arms and rubbing his red eyes. His face looked so innocent, so young suddenly, no longer a man, not even a soldier. Then, back on the bed, he began to hit her again, harder this time, harder blows with not his opened palm but his knuckles, on her face, jaw, head. It was working. He'd stop and scratch his arms, rub his eyes, maybe remembering the symptoms or maybe just irrevocably nailed to the moment she'd devised. Time for door number three.

"Go get the water, Virgil," she said in a carefully clear voice, which was hard through a mouth filled with blood. Virgil, Sly's birth name. The water was what he'd been tasked with when his mother was giving a home birth to his sister. His mother died the next day, the memory of all memories "Get the water, Virgil," Berry repeated, feeling like it was the cruelest thing she'd ever said, maybe the cruelest thing she'd ever imagined. He couldn't save his mother during her childbirth screams, so the birthing screams of an Afghani prisoner in the next cell triggered that memory. And Berry had just become a trigger herself.

Now it was Sly huddled in the corner of their bedroom, scratching his arms, rubbing his red eyes almost like the chemical nerve agents had been unleashed in their bedroom. In a way, they had.

Berry Raskin climbed off the bed and limped to the bathroom, careful to not shock herself by looking in the mirror. She was alive, and her wounds would heal, eventually.

"Good night, Virgil. See you on the other side."

THE END

# What Ever Happened To Myriad Tales Online?

## Cory Clark

The 3 Basic Rules of Running ArcheSky OS on your Virtual Reality Supported Distribution System.

As of 1992, upon establishment of the ArcheSky software development suite, there are three major rules that must be followed to ensure proper usage of our company's development suite.

> 1. Every product, no matter if it's a game, commerce website, entertainment website, or framework/mainframe system, all instances of a running ArcheSky system must have a Coordinator AI to manage resources, debug, etc.

2.    Coordinators are exclusively for management, and are not to be hidden from the user's view, nor are they to take on the likeness of celebrities, important figureheads, or other likenesses already established to avoid copyright or defamation.

3. Never, under any circumstance, allow more than one AI to exist in your system. The AI can and will attempt to grow beyond its program, and can have dire consequences.

We'd done it a thousand times before. There was something of a flow to it by this point; her and I saw it forming after our second or so dive. Annette always did have that vigor to her through. As much as she had to lean on me for the real info gathering and logistics, at least I could rely on her to lead the charge and deal with more hazardous situations.

"Where to again? Dad didn't mention anything other than its name being Myriad Tales Online. At least, it didn't seem like he knew himself," I said softly to her, daring not to open my eyes just yet.

She kept silent for a bit before loudly saying, "That's because he doesn't! His whole job is just sending us to some God-forsaken spit of cyberspace in some dark, desolate corner of the Old Net!"

"Keep it down!" I growled to her, "You know how pissy he gets when you criticize him."

Annette sighed and replied, "Nick, you know he's probably not even awake at this point."

A sharply pitched droning noise started humming its way to my ears, meaning we had about thirty seconds left.

"Still, I can't say I'm exactly happy to be sent this far out into the Old Net without even an idea of what to expect," I accidentally thought aloud, something Annette giggled in response to.

Just as I thought the coast was clear, I opened my eyes, a second too soon and was met with the hideously bright light of digital noise, like a blinding screen of TV static.

I quickly yelped and started rubbing my eyes, hearing my sister snickering next to me.

"Every single time we do a dive," Annette said between giggles, "you do it every single time."

"Why are these stupid cyberspace helmets able to replicate pain?!" I shouted.

Barely opening my eyes, I could already see a lot of drab gray and muted greens. Once the blur left though, I was far more confused than anything. Putting a hand on the slab of ground, I could feel a sensation of grass despite the entire slope here being one giant pane of crudely-colored, low-resolution textures.

"Did this thing not load right?"

Making several motions with her hands as she fussed with her gear's settings, she replied, "Nope. It's made to look this way for some reason. Pretty! In a weird, old-school way."

I shook my head with a grimace, still working at some of the blurriness in my vision.

"Looks like a courtyard in a castle," I said, aimlessly looking around, "I remember hearing about a lot of games like this, but this is the first time I've seen one for myself."

"Dad played them a lot in college. Never mentioned any of them that looked like this though."

It wasn't too odd to see the occasional dive-game show up on the Old Net, but we knew where most of these little video games were at. Either someone powered on an old server still set up to run on the Old Net, or it was set to turn on at a specific point.

"Nick, come here!"

I hadn't even looked away from her for more than a minute and Annette was already leaning far enough out the window to fall out. I hurried over, pulled her back in and gazed out of the window.

"It's huge, ain't it?" said Annette, poking her head in as much as she could to look out at it with me.

There was quite a large city below, all still done in this blocky, low-resolution style that the castle had. There was a chapel, blacksmith, farmer's market, and quite a bit else down there.

"All I see is a long, long mission for today," I replied, pulling my head back and dusting off bits of pixellated dust from my short, brown hair. I could see a door a bit further in the courtyard from us.

"You always say that," said Annette, playing with her golden locks of hair dangling at her shoulder.

I immediately started walking toward it, saying over my shoulder, "Let's get started then. Sooner we get started, sooner we can call it a day."

With Annette traveling alongside me, we went down a long flight of torchlit stairs, arriving not far from the farmer's market. There really was something eerie about seeing somewhere that'd normally be brimming with life so drained of it. Blocky, roughly textured fruits adorned simple wooden shelves and containers, all of them quiet and still except one.

"Who's there?" I asked sharply, eyes watching a shadow move behind one of the fruit stalls.

"Nick, there ain't a thing there," said Annette, "Gotta

drop the tension little bro; we can't afford to spook the locals."

I raised a brow toward her and asked, "What locals?"

Shrugging her shoulders she said, "Just about every dive-game of this era has to at least have a Coordinator seeing to this place. So maybe if we find the Coordinator, we find the people, right?"

"Which would make sense, everything developed around 2004 would've been using the resident AI system ArcheSky enforces, even these older looking online games. Still, depending on if their AI went screwy, we could have a mystery tracking down the Coordinator. There's also the problem if there's more than--"

"Found the tavern!" shouted Annette, darting off to a rugged looking building with green roof tiles.

I sighed and whispered to myself, "And there she goes, just like in college."

Still, if there would be any life, it'd be where there's almost always a party.

Stepping inside, I could smell the froth of a hearty ale, and while I personally was quite interested in grabbing a pint, I didn't see a soul inside to serve it to me.

"Not even at the Tavern? The hell did everyone go?"

"I don't know, but I'm too sober to start looking," replied Annette, hopping over the bar for some self-serve booze.

"Doesn't this technically count as drinking on the job?" I asked her.

She shrugged and replied, "Dad's asleep, there's nothing monitoring us, and it's been two weeks since we got to enjoy an after-mission drink. I can't say I care, and if I'm gonna go looking for people-"

Directly behind me, a voice whispered, "Looking for

someone?"

I immediately jumped with a shiver down my spine, balling up my fist and slamming it into whatever was behind me with a firm impact shortly after my feet touched the ground again.

"Ow!" shrieked the reeling man, decorated in green with a strange green cap, "Is that really the proper way to treat a bard?! Guards! Have this man arrested for assault!"

I held my hands up and walked backward, barely able to eke out an apology.

"Hey now! You're the one that started this!" shouted Annette from the bar.

Quickly dropping his serious expression, the bard donned a sly smile and said, "Relax blondie, I'm just messing with the kid."

Again, I found myself raising a brow as I dropped my hands to my side. What really threw me for a loop though was that he was just as detailed as I was, meaning he was another Web-Diver that somehow knew how to get to this place.

"I kinda had that coming," said the bard, holding on to the left side of his jaw, "but damn, you have one hell of a left hook."

"Dad trained him well," said Annette, approaching with two glasses of beer and handing me the extra. "So do you know where the Coordinator is?"

"Coordinator?" asked the bard, holding on to his shady smile, "I am but a humble bard; I only coordinate music and lyrics! I can't say I'd ever have need to know someone with such a dour and vapid title."

I sighed and said, "Can we cut the theatrics?"

He gave me a shocked look and said, "Well then! I suppose I'll take my leave if you're going to be that rude to my well-thought-out response!"

By the time he was out of the door, Annette was already catching up, saying to him, "Sorry, he's a little grouchy from lack of alcohol; you know how it is."

I opted to keep my mouth shut for the time being. I was already exhausted trying to figure out why the hell a place like this is even still running in the Old Net. Then again, Dad wouldn't have sent us this way without a good reason, and I suspect he knew whoever set this one up, assuming he didn't do it himself and just didn't feel like combing through it for the goods.

"I suppose I can relate," said the bard. "Now just what brings you to the humble kingdom of Myriad?"

"Consider us something of a welfare check, just making rounds, talking to the big man or woman in charge and seeing if everything's alright in this little corner of the universe," lied Annette sweetly.

"An odd request, but sadly this humble bard would only know the little people around town."

Annette slumped her shoulders a bit.

"But if anyone would know how to reach out to the king, or Coordinator, or whomever of importance in this little kingdom, the blacksmith would."

Any lead was better than relying on this bard to guide us around. He was even kind enough to guide us to the blacksmith's workshop, where the glow of smoldering steel and fleeing sparks illuminated an outdoor smithy.

Just as the bard was about to depart from our party, I looked him in the eyes and said, "Hey, I don't think we ever caught your name."

He smiled that roguish smile again, saying, "Reginald. It was a pleasure adventurers, and best of luck to you."

I still couldn't bring myself to trust him. It's an awfully

big coincidence that a server offline for this long suddenly pops back online and he knows exactly when it does and exactly where it is. Any attempt to look up his Dive Info was met with a privacy screen that kept me from seeing anything, leaving me with a strong desire to keep an eye on him. It's not the first time I've seen server owners shield their beloved AIs like this, and it makes it all the more irksome when they play the fool.

"Few things more fun than filtering through rabid role-players that have spent way too much time stewing in the medieval tea. Gonna take the whole day to figure out where the hell the Coordinator is at this rate." I remarked to myself quietly, thinking aloud.

We arrived at the blacksmith's workshop, clad in rough cobblestone and wooden struts. As with Reginald, the blacksmith had an appearance indistinguishable from me or Annette, making him our second Web-Diver we've come across here. From the sweat dripping down his gently tanned face, working its way down his black beard, to his slightly scorched overalls, he looked just as real as us.

"Hail, young adventurers!" bellowed the blacksmith. "What brings you to my shop? In need of a blade?"

Before he could continue pitching his wares, I interrupted him with a simple question.

"Would you happen to know how to contact the Coordinator of this server?"

He reared back in shock like he was legitimately surprised I decided to skip the dialogue and get right to my question of choice.

"A mighty bold request, but I'm afraid I don't have contact with any Coordinator," he replied with a disheartened expression. "Not anymore anyways."

"Wait, so you did at one point?"

He grunted and said, "Closest thing I can recommend is the local king, but he's not accepting visitors at the moment since he's too busy. I reckon if you really wanted to though, you can handle some of his work; that might free him up some."

Crossing my arms with a sigh, I asked, "What did you have in mind?"

The blacksmith pointed a finger to a distant cave, visible from the city gates.

"Dragon's been bothering the town for quite a while," he gruffly replied.

I looked at Annette and said, "It's a lead, but I'm still wanting to tail that bard. There's no guarantee this 'king' would know anything, or he'd try dodging the question like everyone else around here likes to do."

"But the king would be the better choice for gathering direct intel! You can't go rushing headlong into assumptions, Nick. He could very well be the Coordinator we're looking for," said Annette.

I didn't even realize I was halfway to scowling when Annette nudged my arm. I snapped out of my decision-making trance just long enough to see the blacksmith looking at us with a much calmer, friendlier expression.

"You know what I do when I struggle to make a decision?" asked the blacksmith.

We both gave him empty looks for a second, prompting him to head back into his home. He retrieved a bag that clicked and clacked with every wiggle.

"I let Lady Luck decide for me."

Pulling out a twenty-sided die decorated in a gleaming, almost obsidian-like color and etched with bright-white chalk numbers, he tossed it in his hands a few times before rolling it.

"High numbers for the first option, low for the second," he said, waiting patiently for the now-spinning die to finally settle into a number.

After a few seconds of spinning, it stuttered and eventually stopped with the number 12 facing skyward.

I gave a shrug and said, "Guess that's as good as a decision-maker as any."

"Thank you!" Annette said with a beaming smile.

Picking up the die, he threw it over to me, surprising me and causing me to nearly drop it.

"Keep one on hand. Never know when you'll need to let luck lead the way," said the blacksmith.

Annette grabbed me swiftly by the wrist and took off, forcing me to follow suit.

Once we were past the city gates, I snapped my wrist back and asked, "Okay, what's gotten into you?"

Keeping her smile strong, she marched along without a response until we got to the cave.

"Uh, Annette? Is it really wise to just wander into the cave of a dragon like this? I know we can't actually die in any of these worlds, but-"

"What dragon?" asked Annette.

It took me a moment to realize we were just in a giant brown expanse of the same blocky backgrounds, just with less light.

"None of this is making sense. What the hell is going on here?" I asked her.

"I've got a few theories, but nothing concrete yet, so stay tuned!" jested Annette, making her best effort to investigate despite the low lighting.

I could hear a loud bell toll from the church in town, making me jump. Thinking about it, that was one of the places we hadn't checked yet.

"I'm heading back over to the church. Hopefully I can find somebody that can leave behind the role-playing for five minutes and catch me up on what's going on in this place," I said to Annette, my voice echoing far into the enormous cave.

"'Kay!"

But when I got back to the city, I could see from the gate that the glow from the blacksmith's furnace was gone, and the door was shut tight with a sign that said, "Out for materials. Be back soon."

Quickly casting it out from my mind, I narrowed my focus to the church, just a short walk from the blacksmith's workshop. Once I got there, again, I saw an unfortunate sign hanging from the door.

"Pastor Axaria is currently out. If youneed assistance, please contact Reginald Everwind."

Aggravated, I attempted to force open the door, stumbling forward when I realized it wasn't even locked in the first place. Quickly regaining my footing, I took a look around to see if anyone was inside, shutting the door behind me and locking it for good measure.

There wasn't much inside of note, just the normal church pews, the podium in the back, and some chairs, but something stuck out of the trashcan nearby that definitely warranted my attention.

"Brave band of heroes slay resident dragon pest," I read the paper aloud.

A lot of the details weren't even filled in, and any information that was filled in was hastily covered up with ink.

"Reginald Everwind, Thyllius Starglaive, and Pastor Axaria banded together to conquer the mighty dragon that's been causing havoc for the city ever since it woke from hibernation, with King-"

I couldn't make out anything past that; there was too much ink stain.

My scowl was in full force as I muttered to myself, "Goddamned blacksmith sent us on a wild goose chase to give us the slip. Great, now I've got two suspects missing and no clue where they could've gone."

A sudden jostling of the locked door made me jump, leading me to look around for some spot to hide. No closets and no room under the pews made me turn to the rafters, where a few support beams were just within reach if I used a nearby bookshelf. Clambering up and feeling some approximation of digital wood on my hands, I quickly hid up in the shadows near the entrance of the church.

All that effort getting into position would come to nothing, as the rattling stopped and several minutes ran by.

"Was that Annette looking for me maybe?"

With nowhere to go, I had to rely on the sole upper window to check and see if anyone was at the door. It didn't look like there was anyone hovering near the door, so after a few seconds, I hopped down and unlocked the door. I walked backward with the door in hand so anyone there wouldn't see me immediately.

After a few seconds, I deemed the way clear and ducked out of the church. The next step was to scour the town to either find the bard or the blacksmith to force out some answers.

It still didn't feel right walking down city streets where there wasn't a soul to be seen. I'm so used to popping into one of these games and not being able to see two feet in front of you with how densely packed they were.

But not here. There wasn't any background music, something I'm guessing probably didn't load properly, so the only thing I could hear was the whistling of the wind growing ever louder the more I wandered around town.

Opening the tavern doors was met with a rigid creaking, followed by nothing at all, not even the wind anymore. No sign of green bard duds or his blonde ponytail anywhere.

"Where else?" I pondered aloud.

There was that incident over at the farmer's market I could revisit. But I'd also left Annette alone for quite a while now, something Dad tried to stress not to do. He's far too protective of her though. I've worked with her for years and she usually doesn't step out of line.

Fishing out that twenty-sided dice that the blacksmith gave me, I said to myself, "Highs, I go to the market. Lows, I find that sister of mine."

I gave it a gentle throw along a long table, watching it waste no time homing in on the number twelve.

"Farmer's market it is," I said to myself.

The moment I opened the door and took a step out, I could hear something move in the very back of the Tavern. I stood for a solid five minutes watching every shadow in the depths of the Tavern, but nobody reared their head nor responded to my shouts for a response.

*This place gives me the creeps; I'm ready to get the hell out of here"* I thought to myself.

It didn't seem like anything else had been disturbed over at the market. Everything was still exactly where it was supposed to be, in all its blocky, chunky glory.

But then I saw a slightly jostled fruit stand with a little piece of paper hidden away.

It said: Gave them their first test run today. Put the

usual three up against the dragon; they worked just as flawlessly as I expected, bickering included. It was a good laugh, but when all was said and done, I couldn't bring myself to respawn the dragon. Sean made that and I just couldn't bring myself to keep looking at it.

With a brow raised, I asked myself, "Who the hell is Sean? Is that the real name of one of the two other players here?"

It was then that I heard music coming from somewhere farther away, near the courtyard of the castle. It was some horrendous playing, but if there was even a hint of life around, I was going to find it. I'd had enough at this point and wound up in a sprint for the castle. So much crap had gone off the rails from this adventure that I didn't even care who I found up there. One of those other Divers was going to spill the details one way or another.

Flying up gray brick stairs and charging through the courtyard, I arrived at the massive brown door that marked the entrance to the castle. Flinging it open, I was greeted with an empty throne and a complacently smiling Annette.

"Took you long enough," she said with a giggle, putting down the lyre she had been playing.

Giving an exhausted sigh, I said to her, "Answers. Now."

"Perhaps I would, in fact, be better suited to that command," said a familiar voice behind me.

I jumped a bit, angrily responding, "How about you quit sneaking up on people first?!"

"My, my, is that any way to talk to the newfound king of Myriad Online?"

All I could do was stare as I tried piecing things together.

"Come on, can't make it that easy," joked Annette, "Come on Nick, I know this is all a bit much."

We walked over to a long table where a grand feast of bits and bytes awaited, alongside our missing blacksmith.

"Long time no see," jested the blacksmith. "Suppose this is as good a time as any to introduce myself. I'm Thyllius Starglaive, better known as Abe, close friend to your Dad and the lazy bard here."

With the four of us seated toward the end, the bard cleared his throat and downed some wine before speaking.

"I am the current king of Myriad, having taken the role of king after the previous king logged off and never came back. That king was none other than Tavus Scott."

"Remember Dad's old friend he always talked about, the one he hung out with a lot in high school?"

Narrowing my gaze at her, I said, "Yeah, that sure dwindles down the possibilities. The man has hundreds of friends he talks about."

I did vaguely recall Tavus being mentioned though. It was someone Dad had a lot of respect for, but they scarcely talked since high school.

Crossing my arms and keeping my gaze narrowed, I said to Annette, "While this is all nice, this still doesn't explain where the Coordinator is. We have to know where he is to get server access."

Holding a hand out to Reginald, Annette replied, "You're looking at 'im."

I did not like where this was going at all.

"Humans are not allowed to be the Coordinator under any circumstance, what do you-"

"Easy kid!" Reginald cut me off. "Look, this isn't a great solution by my standards either. I don't agree with Tavus' choice on this matter, but I assure you, there's reasons for what's happening here."

"There used to be twelve of us here," Abe finally spoke up, "but friends get busy. They leave. And many don't come back. Tavus didn't like that much, and did the unspeakable. He remade several of us as AI based on the Coordinator's schematics."

My eyes widened and I said fiercely, "Did he have any idea the implications of such an act?!"

"He did," Annette said firmly. "This wasn't a decision either of these two asked for. But Tavus couldn't bear to lose any other friends to time and responsibilities. I can't say I really blame him."

"Annette, the whole reason the Old Net has been separated from modern internet systems is because of rogue AI like this." I said, shifting my glare to Reginald. "I'm going to need the server administration account access immediately."

"Now let's not get hasty," he replied.

I refused to cease my glare, but kept quiet.

"Reginald, maybe it's time to finally let go," said Abe, "Tavus is gone. He's been gone for, hell, years now, and most of the others had to be deleted when their AI started freaking out. What's really worth keeping here besides a bunch of broken memories?"

For once, Reginald slumped in his chair, softly shaking his head.

Not even bothering to look over to me, he said, "I leave the decision up to you. I make no excuse for what Tavus did. Just keep in mind the memories are still here. The people still here."

I gripped the die he gave me in my hand, finally bringing it out.

"I'm at a loss here," I said aloud, giving a long sigh

afterward. "Screw it. Highs the server stays until we can reconvene with Dad. Lows, we're shutting this whole thing down."

Giving it a hearty throw, it bounced a bit before spinning like a top with a good amount of energy.

It was hard to think about what a place like this meant to Tavus, or even Dad. I guess looking at it, this was the closest thing some of these people had to a home. Knowing Dad's history, he probably has his own share of memories tucked away.

The top slowed down, losing momentum, and just as it was about to hit the table, I stopped it with a flat palm. With all of the numbers obscured, I slowly put it back in my pocket.

"I..."

I paused for a second, a hundred infectious motives and thoughts wandering around my head in a densely packed mess.

"I don't feel I'm at liberty to make the call on this. Dad needs to be the one to handle this one."

As harsh as the repercussion I'd face for going against orders, I really didn't know how to approach this. This was something training didn't cover.

"A good choice," said Annette. "I think our duty is done here for the moment. Shall we head back?"

I nodded, tapping the temple of my head twice to bring up the user interface so I could log out of the Dive Gear and head back into the real world.

"It was great meeting you both!" said Annette, bringing up her interface. "I promise I'll come back. I wanna hear more stories about you all and Dad!"

"Take care little one," said Reginald with a bright smile.

Abe kept quiet as we left, looking to us with a somber

gaze.

The transition back to reality is far smoother than when we head into one of those worlds. Dad was waiting patiently for us, his stony, chiseled face looking at us like a General to his army.

"So, what all happened?"

"A lot of ArcheSky violations is what happened. AI dressed up to look like other Divers, a Coordinator and other AI that look like deceased people. All of this probably of no surprise to you, right Dad?"

He looked at me with his hardened expression before finally dropping the facade.

"Cameras are already turned off Dad, ain't anyone listening right now," said Annette casually, "If you're gonna speak your mind, time to do it."

"I'm-" Dad paused for a moment. "I'm sorry for what I did. I shouldn't have sent you two in to clean up my loose ends. But I'm sure you already know the answer to your question."

"What question?" I asked.

"Of whether or not to shut down that server, of course."

I kept silent for the moment, while Dad went to his jet-black modern desk, opening up a drawer and pulling out a bag and a little wooden instrument.

Handing the little instrument to Annette, she immediately started fussing with it, playing it all the while, just as Reginald showed her.

Dad handed me the bag, a bag that made very distinct clicking and clattering sounds. Quickly opening it, I had a very familiar black die in my hand. A die that had twenty sides, all with the same number on it.

"Not a very useful die," I remarked.

"Abe always had trouble making decisions. He believed

in fooling himself first and foremost, finding ways to work around the indecisiveness. Truth is, he always knew which decision was the right one and always placed his bets on the decision he wanted it to be."

"So what, was Reginald just a theater nerd or something?" asked Annette, still playing the little lyre.

Dad laughed and said, "It was his namesake. Hell, we rarely even called him by name, just 'The Bard'. He always had a way of inspiring people with music. He knew what to play and when to play it, and everyone always felt better after listening. But for all the listening he did to his own music, he never wanted to face the music others brought to him."

After an uncomfortable silence, I asked, "What happened to them?"

As Dad's face twisted back into that heartless, cold expression, he finally replied, "Abe died in a car crash seven years ago, and Reginald came up as a missing persons case shortly after Pastor Axaria was convicted of three counts of manslaughter."

Annette stopped playing with the lyre immediately, and I hung my mouth in disbelief.

"Kids. I think it's about time to go visit Tavus. It's been a bit too long," said Dad rapidly.

It was a bit hard to think about a road trip after that bombshell, but Dad was rather insistent, and I needed some fresh air anyway to work out the emotions wandering around in my head. It wasn't but a few moments after our shift ended that we packed up for a long, four hour journey. Bumpy roads, crappy weather, a very angry moose and a frozen-over lake later, and we were in a cold, lightless spit of land far up north.

What we found in his house brought us no joy or

pleasure. What we found was a corpse. One that had been long dead and rotting. The reports labeled it as a suicide by overdose, but Dad refused to believe that. He wanted to push the envelope, insist that something wasn't right in this case and we'd be needing that old server for answers.

We were just data recovery specialists for ArcheSky, our only directives for doing Old Net dives were to go in, grab the important information, then shut the server down. We had no authority to investigate a potential murder.

Yet, to this day, that server, the fortress of stagnation that Tavus filled with broken laws and far more broken memories, remains online. And we had one hell of a time explaining this to the higher-ups.

Hence why we're now running for our lives.

# ABOUT THE AUTHORS

## Timothy Baldwin

Timothy Baldwin grew up in Syracuse, New York. He currently resides in Maryland where he teaches English, Creative Writing, Film, and Theatre on the middle school level. At the insistence of his own students, he began writing seriously in 2014.

He credits his love for stories to his mother, who spent countless hours reading to him and his siblings when they were growing up. Growing up, he devoured the literary words of C. S. Lewis, J. R. R. Tolkien, Piers Anthony, and many others. Mysteries, thrillers, and fantasies are among the genre he most frequently reads. When he's not writing, he's reading, teaching, camping, or enjoying a live music concert.

## Cory Clark

Cory Clark is a small-town writer branching out from an IT background to work on his writing abilities after a long hiatus. When not working on a small gig in gaming journalism, he's working on short stories and his first major novel series, and enjoys writing science fiction with hints of fantasy and mystery.

## Michael Deeze

MICHEAL DEEZE was a child in the notorious Maplewood Commons housing projects of inner city

Chicago, growing up hard. And fast. Surrounded by crime and violence, his family struggled to just hold their own while trying to escape their own poverty. Deeze gained street sense young, and it became the backdrop for a life of multiple indiscretions and occupations, call them what you will.

Deeze is a natural-born storyteller—in life and in print. A child of the sixties, he draws extensively from his own diverse experiences and subsequent education to introduce the hapless Emmett Casey. As U.S. Army veteran and retired Doctor of Chiropractic, Deeze now lives in Illinois after spending decades living near the forests of northern Wisconsin. He's a devoted father to his three children, a magical daughter, two grown sons, and his dog. His first novels are the critically acclaimed Bless Me Father, and For I have Sinned, The Heretic  is the final novel in the series.

## Marie Judson

Marie Judson lives on the wild Northern California coast. An ardent fantasy and sci fi reader since childhood, she also loves singing harmony, working with dreams, and trying to save our planet.

## D. Krauss

D. Krauss resides in the Shenandoah Valley, Virginia. He has been a cottonpicker, a sodbuster, a librarian, a surgical orderly, the guy who paints the little white line down the middle of the road, a weatherman, a door-kickin' shove-gun-in-face lawman, a hunter of terrorists, and a school bus driver. Currently, he's a layabout. He's been married over 45 years (yep, same woman), and has a wildman bass guitarist for a son.

## Ana Manwaring

Ana Manwaring is a former newspaper lifestyle columnist. Her poetry, personal narratives, book reviews and short stories have appeared in diverse publications including the California Quarterly, KRCB Radio, Morning Haiku, Mystery Readers Journal, Stolen Light Ed. Fran Claggett, and Sisters Born, Sisters Found Ed. Laura McHale Holland.

A graduate of the University of Denver (B.A.) in Education and English Lit and Sonoma State University (M.A.) in Education/Linguistics, Ana teaches creative writing in California's wine country, produces the monthly FUNdaMentalists poetry event on Zoom and operates her editing company, JAM Manuscript Consulting—"Spread Excellence." In her "past life," she has owned and operated BookWork, an accounting and tax preparation service, managed a social service non-profit organization serving immigrants, and cared for the elderly, all of which she gave up to work for a PI, consult *brujos*, and out-run gun totin' maniacs on lonely Mexican highways—the inspiration for, *the JadeAnne Stone Mexico Adventures*.

Ana's husband David, ace gopher hunter Alison, and a host of birds, opossums, skunks, deer, fox, coyotes, and occasionally the neighboring goats, co-habitat an acre of Northern California.

After earning her M.A., Ana finally answered her mother's question, "What are you planning to do with that expensive education?" Be a paperback writer.

## Lisa Orban

Lisa Orban was born in Galesburg, IL a long time ago on a hot summer day. Due to various shenanigans by the adults in her life, her time in Galesburg was short and the family moved to Quincy, IL where they settled down for a good long stay.

Things were rolling along for a while inside the

confines of Quincy, and Lisa rolled with them. There were several divorces, marriages, different schools, friends lost & gained, and many, *many* moves throughout all this activity. Until, quite unexpectedly, Lisa found herself in foster care at 16, much to her surprise.

Upon turning 18, Lisa ran away as fast as she could to Phoenix, AZ where she lived for 3 years. Got married, had two sons, made many mistakes, and then eventually, ran for her life back to Quincy, where she still lives to this day.

Lisa went to college, earned an Associates in Psychology, raised her 5 kids, got married, and divorced, several times, bought a house and eventually settled down to live the life she always wanted, as the ringleader in a madhouse of anarchy. She now writes books, takes in human strays in need of help, travels, opened a publishing house, and pretty much does whatever she wants, and is quite happy about it.

## Lisa Towles

Lisa Towles is an Amazon bestselling, award-winning crime novelist and a passionate speaker on the topics of fiction writing, creativity, and self care. She has ten crime thrillers in print with a new title, Terror Bay, forthcoming in November of 2023. Her latest thriller, Salt Island (June, 2023) won both a Readers Choice and a Pencraft literary award. Salt Island is the second book in her E&A Investigations series following Hot House (June, 2022). Lisa is a member of Mystery Writers of America, Sisters in Crime, and International Thriller Writers and is deeply committed to supporting writers' success through friendship, fellowship and community engagement. She is Board President of a Bay Area nonprofit (Bridgegood.org) and speaks frequently to groups of business leaders and writers. She has an MBA in IT Management and works full-time in the tech industry in the San Francisco Bay area.

Thank you for taking the time to read this collection from the authors of Indies United Publishing House. We hope you enjoyed it and would like to encourage you to take a moment to review this collection on your favorite reading platform.

# A little about Indies United

Here at Indies United, we are a co-op of like-minded authors working together to showcase our books and highlight our diversity as writers. We openly encourage and support both new and established authors in their pursuit of finding their audience while bringing to you books worth reading. Our goal is to give authors a home to call their own, while bringing fresh, innovative, and exciting books to readers all over the world.

If you are an author, please check us out at
www.indiesunited.net

www.ingramcontent.com/pod-product-compliance
Lightning Source LLC
Chambersburg PA
CBHW070042130726
47907CB00017B/1347